BLUE LIGHT SPECIAL

JAN ALLINDER ANESTIS

BLUE LIGHT SPECIAL is an original work of fiction. Names, characters, places, and incidents are from my imagination or are used fictionally. Any resemblance to actual places, events, or persons, living, dead, or immortal is entirely coincidental.

BLUE LIGHT SPECIAL Copyright © 2013, Jan Allinder Anestis. All rights are reserved. No part of this book may be used or reproduced in any form whatsoever without prior written permission of the publisher.

Cover design by: Daphne Firos
www.studiofiros.com

ISBN-13: 9781492772187
ISBN-10: 1492772186

Also by Jan Allinder Anestis

MIND OVER MIRROR
A romantic beach read for the bifocal set.
By
Jan Allinder Anestis
Wandaleen Cole, Jack Hailey
Bill McDonald and Jo Ann Walther

ACKNOWLEDGEMENTS

A loving thank you to my sons, Matthew, Mark, and Michael, and to their wives, Gillian, Stephanie, and Joye, who encouraged me to publish BLUE LIGHT SPECIAL; and who, with their precious children, add great happiness to my life.

I also owe thanks to a group of close friends, who read the manuscript through many edits and cheered me on every step of the way; and to Daphne Firos, who almost instantaneously grasped the essence of the story and created a perfect cover.

And a major thank you to my husband, Bob, who makes me laugh most every day, and who has always encouraged me to pursue my dreams.

TABLE OF CONTENTS

Chapter 1	1
Chapter 2	7
Chapter 3	13
Chapter 4	21
Chapter 5	27
Chapter 6	33
Chapter 7	37
Chapter 8	47
Chapter 9	53
Chapter 10	61
Chapter 11	65
Chapter 12	69
Chapter 13	77
Chapter 14	85
Chapter 15	91
Chapter 16	95
Chapter 17	97
Chapter 18	101
Chapter 19	109

Chapter 20	115
Chapter 21	123
Chapter 22	129
Chapter 23	135
Chapter 24	141
Chapter 25	147
Chapter 26	155
Chapter 27	161
Chapter 28	167
Chapter 29	171
Chapter 30	175
Chapter 31	179
Chapter 32	185
Chapter 33	193
Chapter 34	195
Chapter 35	203
Chapter 36	207
Chapter 37	211
Prologue	215
Author Biography	223

CHAPTER 1

I need to focus. Three short weeks – that's how much time I have to accomplish all I want to do. A paltry twenty-one days and twenty-one nights to make Dick dump her and want me. And I'm not talking about an eye for an eye; I want his whole darn body back! But how do I make that happen? That's the question, and sure as I'm standing here, I am not going to figure out the answer by staring at my image in the mirror.

Damn, I do look incredible though. My hair is the color of honey fresh from the hive. Red was nice, audacious even, but this is better. I like the way my hair frames my face. I like my face. I love my butt and my gloriously firm stomach. But most of all, Clarence, thank you, thank you! I adore the cleavage. Breasts rule!

Shoot, there I go again. Ben and Kelly will be ready for breakfast in a few minutes, and I can't stop thinking about how good I look! Hard not to though; it's such a change. I remember how it felt to envy women who look like this. Actually, forget envy. Hate would be a better word. The beautiful ones annoyed me before they uttered a word, but they really irritated me with their pompous pronouncements. Statements like: "Oh, waiter, this is such a large slice of tomato. Would you please box half of it for me to take home for tomorrow's lunch?" And I swear they actually love to exercise.

For example, at a recent Moorestown Young Woman's Club luncheon, I was scarfing down a huge chicken salad and bemoaning my weight. The woman seated beside me took a teensy bite of a carrot stick, looked at me with condescending scorn poorly disguised as empathy, and offered: "You should try biking. I ride my bicycle 45 minutes every morning before breakfast. I also do an additional hour of aerobic and weight training activity in the evening."

Well, didn't that just make me want to barf! (I bet she did that every day too.)

Oh sure she had a point about exercise. I wasn't drop dead gorgeous and I knew it, but who is at forty-three? Even flat-chested and pudgy looked better before the years worked their sinister magic. But that was before I met Clarence. Bless him! I said I needed bigger boobs and a firm ass, and look at me!

There I go again, babbling on about my appearance, instead of focusing on the task at hand. So, here's my plan: I'll make some coffee and then I will explain the outrageously ridiculous, right out of a Stephen King nightmare details. No hysterics, just a calm and orderly presentation of the sorry tale of my life as Mrs. Clueless. Then maybe I can figure out exactly what I have to do to reclaim what belongs to me.

Oh, just a quick comment before I continue. My name is not, and never was Mrs. Clueless. If you thought that really was my name, even for a split second, perhaps you better reevaluate your decision to listen to my sordid saga. It gets way trickier from here.

With that warning, here goes: I never imagined I would have to say this, but my life as Beatrice Marie Kelly McBane took a serious detour from Happyville. In fact, my life as Mrs. McBane would have been over, done and gone, washed-up, finis, no need for Clarence's ministrations, if not for Jane's interference. I love Jane dearly, but she did screw up my plans.

I can't second guess what I did – I had to call her. Jane has been one of my two best friends since grade school. At forty-two she is still quite cute in a no make-up, every guy's best buddy sort of way. She is creative and spunky, and she has an incredible singing voice! In fact, we all thought she was destined for a charmed life on Broadway. I mean, Manhattan is practically our next door neighbor. But right smack dab in the middle of our senior year, before Jane managed even one interview, her parents moved to Texas. Yes, you heard right. Gawd-awful Texas!

It might as well have been Outer Mongolia! Nobody we knew had ever moved there, and none of us had the money to visit. Jane was lonely and depressed. To her credit, she tried, but she bombed out at every audition in the land where the antelope play and the buffalo roam. I guess eventually she just gave up on her dreams, and without even asking my opinion, she dropped out of college, married a big burly Texan named Bart, and settled down next door to her folks.

Then six years ago, Jane moved back to Moorestown with her two kids but minus husband Bart. Seems he had ridden off into the sunset with most of their money and all of Jane's self-esteem. So much for the charmed life theory.

But I digress. You don't care about Jane. You want to know about Dick and me. You want the demented details of Dick's dalliance. Rick the prick. Rich and the bitch. Darling depraved Dick. (How absurdly prophetic was his mother's choice of his name?)

I suppose I should start with the day I learned that Dick was involved with another woman. That would be Wednesday, May

29th. I ate lunch with my usual enthusiasm, discovered Dick's extra-curricular activity, and promptly expelled the contents of my stomach. Then I made my fatal mistake. I dialed Jane and told her of my calamitous find and subsequent decision to dump Dick and rediscover life without the burden of hearth and home. I did not ask for advice, mind you. I just wanted to rant and rave a bit to an ear I expected to be receptive to my pain.

Unfortunately I did not consider one significant fact. Jane had been living the single life, and it was not going well.

"Ignore it," she advised. "Pretend it never happened."

"I will not!" I replied, scrunching my face for emphasis.

"You'll regret it," she insisted.

"I won't. You may regret the loss of your husband, but I am not you." I spit the words at her, aware they would hurt.

I heard Jane swallow. "Fine," she said, acknowledging my verbal victory. That victory that was short lived, however, because Jane pulled the perfect power play. She dashed over to Saint Mary's and blabbed to our parish priest.

Before God's hit man entered the equation, I considered my marriage all but officially over. Then the phone rang. His summons was firm and curt. "Beatrice? My office, half-past three," he said and immediately hung up.

Of course, I anticipated resistance to the idea of divorce, but I was prepared to counter any objection. I strode into his study, sobbed out the details of my discovery, and sat back to accept compassionate advice on how to erase Dick from my life.

"How can I stay with a man who would do that?" I asked him, after a good hardy sob.

I expected him to fume and seethe about Dick's behavior. Seriously, the big "A" is a sin most mainstream Catholics frown on. Hell, it even made the original Top Ten List. However, his holiness buzzed right past "thou shalt not commit adultery" and zeroed in on the effects of divorce on children, and then the pompous penguin had the nerve to remind me of my own for better or for worse vow, declaring that my immortal soul was at risk if I did not cooperate with his save-the-marriage plan.

That did it. Despite my original resolve to divorce the beast I married 22 years before, the combination of destroying my children's lives and casting my soul into hell was daunting. I made one last valiant effort to reason with the good father, and then I caved and agreed to his plan of action.

"You will not regret this, Beatrice," he proclaimed smugly as he listed his plan: reflect daily on my relationship with Dick; look at my own contributions – good and bad – to our marriage; and refrain from purposeless digs at the filthy little tart – oops, excuse me – I mean at Dick's *temptation,* as the good Father so delicately christened her.

"It is probably best to limit your meditation to three times a day," he added cheerfully as I shuffled out of his office.

Infuriating as the situation itself was, Father Tom's rules were more so. Therefore, I developed my own guidelines. I would be as vindictive about Dick's trashy little trollop as I wished; and I would perform Father Tom's irritating ritual not thrice but once a day, immediately before dinner. I figured if my luck improved - and how could it not - reflecting on the years I wasted with Dick might kill my appetite. Then I'd accomplish something truly meaningful, like losing a pound or two before the Lord of Hosts High School Class of 1988's twenty fifth reunion.

Too bad I did not know about Clarence's talents, I would have changed my rule to: meditate after dinner while consuming quart of rum raisin ice cream. Great body will follow in God's own time.

CHAPTER 2

Before I donned my virginal garb to stand before God and the angels of holy matrimonial bliss to become legally linked to dastardly Dick, my maiden name was Beatrice Marie Kelly. I was raised in a by-the-rules Irish Catholic home. Birth control was a sin, and if mom's eggs had cooperated, there would have been at least a dozen of us. Thankfully a lower than average fertility rate and two miscarriages interceded. Still mom and dad managed to produce five daughters. Seven of us squeezed into a three-bedroom, two-bath, split-level, and as the youngest, I had last call more often than not.

If life at home was crowded and depressing, the outdoors provided relief. We lived in a gentle neighborhood where children could play without fear. There I forged a bond with my best friends Jane and Lorna, who dubbed me Beanie sometime shortly after they developed the glorious protrusions that I never did sprout. For I, in true Kelly tradition, was indubitably under-endowed, voluptuously-challenged, flat as the plains in Toto's home state.

I suppose there is a silver lining to my boyish physique, for if I had not been so dismally stacked, I might have remained unaware of Dick's extra-curricular activities. I might well have continued on for years obliviously happy.

But I did not remain either oblivious or happy. On that fatal May afternoon, while gathering laundry, I discovered a lavishly wrapped package in Dick's gym bag, obviously a birthday gift for my up-coming forty-third birthday. Forty-frigging-three – well on my way down the slippery slope toward fifty.

I was not at all happy about that birthday. I did not want to be forty-three or any of the numbers after that, because I'd already glimpsed the future and it did not look good! For instance, I recently had to switch from semi-permanent to permanent hair color because the gray hairs sprouting wildly in my once gloriously auburn mop no longer responded to a milder solution. Worse yet, after decades of two-piece bathing suits, I had graduated to a one-piece with a high Spandex content.

So given my pre-birthday emotions – depressed, restless, irrational, bitchy – I was certain Dick would want to buy me the perfect gift, something to give me a much-needed psychological lift up and out of the doldrums. Unfortunately, Dick was a dismal failure in the gift buying department. The only jewelry he ever bought unguided was a sterling silver ID bracelet for my penicillin allergy; and last year's birthday gift was a heavy-duty chrome blender. I figured if this year's item was too grotesque to live with, that I could drop hints about not wanting whatever it was before he gave it to me – a less embarrassing experience for Dick, I reasoned, than rejecting his offering after the fact.

Sufficiently rationalized, I carefully separated the tape from the black and silver paper, took a deep breath and ignoring all twinges of anxiety, slid the box out of its covering, and lifted the lid.

I gently caressed the tissue paper that was folded delicately across the contents. It was rather titillating, the combination of sneaking a look at what I wasn't meant to see and wondering if I might find something intriguing concealed within that box.

Well, I found something intriguing all right. No blender. Just sexy black silk lingerie. And almost as soon as I saw the contents, I knew those lacy delicacies were not meant for me.

The thong was sized to fit a firm little derriere, one with pelvic bones that had never been displaced giving birth to a nine-pound baby. I stared at its skimpiness in disbelief. Then I turned the bra over and squinted at the tag. 32DD! If my bottom had cleavage to spare, my top made the American grasslands look mountainous. Hell, my nursing bras had been smaller than most training bras.

To make matters worse, while I briefly entertained the irrational hope that size aside, those sexy garments were meant for me, all fantasies were destroyed when I discovered the note tucked into the bra. It read:

Mercedes, this will look perfect on you, and the lace should stretch comfortably over your nipple-ring.

Love, Your Dickie.

I stared at the note. I could think of two things named Mercedes. One was Mercedes Alverez, an ever-so-perky young woman, who had worked as a student teacher in Dick's classroom four or five years ago. The other was a vintage convertible coupe that Dick had coveted since he saw it at the Moorestown Classic Car Gallery. I doubted he was buying underwear for a car.

And he'd signed the note Dickie! The man is forty-six years old. Even his mother, a freeze-dried debutante from Cherry Hill, doesn't call him Dickie.

Maybe there is an innocent explanation, I thought, as waves of nausea propelled the half-digested bits of chicken tacos into my throat. Perhaps Dick has a friend named Dickie, a callous cad who asked my sensible, thoughtful Richard to keep the wretched present for him. Or perhaps the gift really is for me, and Dick not only thinks me as a voluptuous sports model, but also believes I am daring enough for the nipple ring he has also purchased.

"Oh come on! You fainted when you had your ears pierced, Beatrice Marie," the damn internal voice of reason that invariably spoiled my fun during my dating years scoffed. "You would never pierce anything else, and Dick knows it. Face it. There is no way that bra is for you."

It has to be a mistake, I told myself. There would have been other signs if Dick were involved with someone else.

I stuffed the package back into Dick's gym bag and dropped it onto the closet floor. Then I stood and took a deep breath. It's cold in here, I thought. My arms and legs shook in agreement.

I stumbled downstairs, stood in the doorway to Dick's study and stared at a desk covered with papers and trophies. The cleaning woman dusted and ran the sweeper, but the room was Dick's to clutter as he saw fit. I had my desk in the kitchen and he had his study; both respected as private. No longer. I searched through desk drawers. I logged onto his computer. By the end of the second hour, I had unearthed enough evidence to convict. Receipts, letters, e-mails. All there. All damning. Why did he save it all? Did he imagine himself impervious to discovery?

I returned to our bedroom. No shaking legs. Anger has its own heat. I opened Dick's closet and stuffed as many of his clothes as I could fit into a suitcase. Then I carried the suitcase and gym bag, complete with lingerie and Dickie's eloquent note, to my car. When I reached the high school faculty parking lot, I wedged both suitcase and gym bag into the front seat of Dick's car. I am proud to report that I resisted the urge to slam my car into the back of his. Admittedly, scratching the letter M with my car key on the car door was childish, but supremely satisfying.

Task completed, I called Jane, who turned me in to Father Tom, who psychologically handcuffed me to hearth and home.

On my way back home from Saint Mary's, I stopped at my other best buddy's house to whine.

"Damn it Lorna, I cannot believe my idiot priest is demanding an introspective cooling-off period before he will even discuss ending our farce of a marriage!" I screamed.

Lorna rolled her eyes and threw up her arms in a gesture of righteous indignation worthy of a pure blooded, from-the-womb, Catholic or Jew. According to Lorna, priests and rabbis have one over-riding ambition – to ruin our lives. Of course she is incredibly negative about religious rules and rituals, having converted to Judaism when she married Irving, a decision she has lamented from day one – converting, that is, not her marriage to Irving.

"I grew up Unitarian," Lorna mused to the air behind my head as she hugged me. "The only time I heard the word sin uttered, was when a woman refused to host coffee hour. No other rules seemed unbendable. Now I am living with a man who has to eat his food from different plates, and you are charged with responsibility for everyone's immortal souls. Let's run away from home!"

I reminded her that it wasn't like the old days when she, Jane, and I would escape to each other's bedrooms to sob out our agonies or proclaim our victories, almost all of which concerned the opposite sex. Every thought, every dream, every fear was presented and examined as we passed them back and forth with great care. The three bears our parents called us, and anyone who tried to hurt one of us knew that a sleuth of bears could be a formidable opponent.

Unfortunately our lives had become much more complicated. If we ran now, we would have to take my kids and her six-year-old beastie twins with us, and of course Jane and her two teenagers would want to come as well. "What kind of escape would that be?" I asked.

Instead I hugged Lorna goodbye, drove home, climbed into bed with a pint of black cherry chocolate chunk ice cream and called it a day.

CHAPTER 3

I assumed the worst moment of my life occurred when I found the strumpet's gift and that things would improve rapidly as soon as everyone rallied around my tortured soul. I was wrong.

The troops did rally. In fact they rallied night and day, but for a different cause than I had anticipated. I could almost hear them chanting as they waved their pompoms to and fro: It's all-ri-ight. It's okay. He'll come back if you just stay!

What a crock! Even Mother Theresa's saintly patience would have collapsed in the fray. I suffered through numerous conversations with Dick's mother, who believed all would be well if I just looked the other way while Dick found himself. My parents believed all would be well if Dick and I entered counseling and found each other; and my sisters believed all would have been well in the first place, if any one of them had found Dick before he married me.

I was also treated to tidbits of biblical and psychological wisdom from various friends and relatives, and of course from the infamous Father Tom. The only person I did not exchange words with was Dick. Words just could not make it past the congealed mass of taco bits that seemed perpetually stuck in my throat.

My parents were beside themselves. (Scary vision: two identical sets of parents, wringing their hands and torturing me with advice about obligation and reputation.) Mom could not complete a full sentence without crying and dad specialized in clearing his throat and patting her on the shoulder. And they were always at the house! On the third day they arrived with enough casseroles for a small funeral reception, so I asked Mom if she thought I should change into something black and cover the mirrors.

"Oh, Beatrice, don't be mean," mom sniffed. "We only want to help."

After another hour with the two of them talking and me mumbling about not really wanting to talk, mom went off to the bathroom to repair her make-up before Ben and Kelly arrived home from school.

Dad hurried to fill the blessed silence created when mom left the living room. "You need to be sensible, Beabums," he said, using his pet name for me. "You have to think of Ben and Kelly."

"I am thinking of them," I assured him, "otherwise your soon to be ex-son-in-law would require the attention of an undertaker with creative embalming skills in order to reconnect the body part I severed while offing him."

I meant my answer to be funny, but dad turned bright red, shook his head, and walked out onto the porch to wait for his grandchildren.

I made a mental note to remember that answer when I wanted to stop others from chattering on endlessly about what I should or should not do. Nothing else seemed to work. Most people seemed too fixated on preventing me from leaving Dick to listen to my reasons for doing just that.

"How come everyone but Lorna finds it amazing that I want to divorce Dick?" I asked Father Tom when he called that Sunday. (I had eluded him after Mass.)

"Are they afraid I cannot take care of myself or provide for my children? Do they really think I should just pretend everything is wonderful?"

"Those, Beatrice, are good questions for you to reflect upon," he answered.

I considered commenting on the brilliance of his answer but he did not handle sarcasm well, and I feared that if provoked, he might add some new *must or must not do* to my list.

"I expect they simply want you to acknowledge that there are still worthwhile aspects to your union." He paused and I guessed that a sermon would follow. I was right.

"Marriage is a sacred commitment in the Catholic faith," he continued. "Right now you think Dick's behavior gives you the right to abdicate your own vows of commitment, but before you set your mind on leaving, you need to better understand the relationship you want to terminate. How is your process coming?"

How is my process coming? Where did the man hone his spectacular communication skills?

"I've had a touch of thinker's block," I hedged.

"Begin," he instructed. "Begin at the beginning. Think about how you met. Think about what attracted you to Dick in the beginning."

I clutched the phone tightly. Think about how we met? Remember what attracted me to him? That was easy. I first saw Dick after a Saint Joseph's University basketball game. He was a junior majoring in history; his dream to teach and coach, with a heavy emphasis on coaching. Dick did not have to worry about wages or potential for advancement. His ample trust funds would supply all the material goods he could desire. His preferred compensation? To be eternally surrounded by adoring cheerleaders and sweat-covered athletes.

I was a lowly freshman, obliged even with considerable scholarship aid to commute to Philadelphia each day from my Moorestown, New Jersey home. My dream was simple. I wanted never again to share living space or possessions with my four annoying sisters, and any career that would accomplish that was fine with me.

Dating someone like Dick was not on my wish list until I saw him; then it bumped right up to number one. He had sandy brown hair and eyes the color of tropical waters in the final magical seconds before the setting sun inflames the surface. Those eyes caught my attention, but it was his smile that captured my heart. Dick was standing with several of his teammates and their adoring female counterparts. Without warning, he turned his head and looked across the bleachers at me. His smile began with a slight upward turn to his mouth, and then it exploded into a full-blown grin.

I waved weakly and turned to one of my freshman buddies to announce: "I'm breaking-up with Ted."

Ted, formally known as Theodore Haybeck, was my high school sweetheart, and we loved each other as only kids that age can. August after our senior year, just before Ted got into his parents car for the drive west to begin his freshman year at the University of Colorado, he gave me a beautiful gold locket engraved with both our names, and we parted crying.

That fall semester he called me daily; and since I couldn't afford to attend any of his dances or frat parties, he made a special effort to phone during the evening of those events, as if to say: Don't worry, Bea, if you cannot come, I'm not interested in attending the party either. No one could have been sweeter.

A few times over the years I've thought of Ted and wondered what would have happened if he and I had gone to the same college. Would things have been different? Would I have continued to care for him as feverishly as I did in high school? I always reached the same conclusion. Nothing would have changed.

For you see, even though I loved Ted as much as any teenage girl can love a boy, I knew before he left for college that I would never marry him. First of all, he was a Methodist, and I hoped to marry someone who could worship with me in the Catholic Church. More importantly, however, Ted was determined to go to law school. I wanted to spend my life making the world a better place. That did not include marrying someone whose career goals involved benefiting from the ill luck or misdeeds of others.

Oh fine, I lie. Ted did intend to become an attorney, but he wanted to represent the downtrodden and ill-equipped-to-pay types. And while he was not Catholic, he would have converted in a snap, if I asked him to. My reasons were far less admirable. I wanted a life I was not confident Ted would provide. He was too inclined to stop and smell the roses when he should be focusing on the bottom-line.

"You need to put more thought into a career and savings and retirement," I reminded him every time he suggested the two of us might do the happily-ever-after thing.

Ted and I argued about my obsession with planning for the future during all of the years we dated. "Can't you live in the present, Bea?" he would ask. "Can't you just enjoy what you have now? The way I look at it, you can waste a great life waiting for the blue-light special!"

The image was perfect for middle class Gen X'ers. We grew up shopping at K-Mart years before it lost its market share to the newer, flashier mega stores. In our teenage years my friends and I were there at least once a week to shop for make-up, panty hose, costume jewelry, even clothes.

The problem was that we did not leave after purchasing what we needed, because we were hooked on the concept of the blue-light special. We were in fact guilty of wasting hours waiting around to see what might be offered next. "Attention, K-Mart shoppers," a voice eventually would boom out through tinny speakers, and we would stand at attention, hoping the next sentence would contain the words jewelry or cosmetics.

"For the next 10 minutes there will be a blue-light special in the automotive department," the voice might decree on a bad day. Even then we would feel compelled to seek out the mobile stand with its flashing blue light. After all, we might find the perfect gift for our dads or our boyfriends, something never before and never again available at such a low price.

Too many times I resisted the tug of Ted's hand or a whispered promise of how we could spend a little time alone together in his car before he had to drop me off at home. "Ten more minutes," I would insist with stubborn resolve.

"Waste of a beautiful day," he would mumble and leave the store in disgust to wait in his car.

The K-mart image triggered a rush of other more intimate memories. I had no idea what had become of Ted since our breakup. He had neither attended nor even returned his questionnaire when we had our tenth reunion. I looked at the list for this year's celebration. There he was under the yes column: Theodore Haybeck, no spouse or guest listed.

I tried to imagine how he might look. At our tenth all the women looked fairly attractive, with the exception of Rene Richards, who was three days past her due date, and never should have been allowed out of the house in a bright pink maternity dress. It was a different story with the men, a number of whom had already begun to show signs of aging.

Twenty-five years post high school the changes could be dramatic. Would Ted still be thin? Would he wear glasses, have wrinkles? Would he have hair? If he did have hair, would it be gray?

"Are you there, Bea?"

Father Tom's voice startled me, and for a few seconds I was sixteen, back in the confessional booth, and certain that he could read my mind. If he did, he would know that my thoughts had wandered from husband to ex-lover. I mumbled a guilty good bye and lowered the receiver onto the base of the phone.

As I stood there, tears began again. I brushed them off with the back of my hand and stomped my foot. "Stop whining," I admonished myself. "There is no value in *what if*!" Still, I had to wonder whether I should have been so quick to break Ted's heart, because I doubted that he would have been as cavalier as Dick about breaking mine.

CHAPTER 4

The following afternoon the phone and doorbell rang simultaneously. I waited a few moments hoping one or the other would simply stop. No such luck. "Coming," I yelled in the general direction of the front door as I grabbed the phone.

"Hello," I mumbled defensively into the receiver.

"Hey, Bea, it's Lorna."

I breathed a silent prayer of thanksgiving that it was not my dad's sister, who had lectured me on the power of forgiveness for nearly an hour the previous evening, complete with a dramatic "Who among us is innocent enough to throw the first stone?" ending. She declared me rude and hung up without a goodbye after I asked if she'd read that story somewhere or if it was an anecdote from her own experiences.

"Get a grip!" I replied, but only after the dial tone testified to the fact that she could not hear me.

"What's up, Lorna?" I asked into the phone.

"I just was thinking that it's Monday, Bea," she replied. "I wondered if we should talk about final preparations for this weekend's party. That is if you are still up to hosting it?"

"I'm planning on it," I answered. "Compared to the rest of my life, the party sounds easy. Besides, where else could we find last minute that would accommodate so many people other than our lake house? Although, it might be tight, as I hear the attendance list has increased in the past few days. People are probably dying to see how devastated I will look."

"You'll look just fine!"

"You think so? Well we'll see how I look with Dick in the same room," I said glancing in the mirror over the buffet.

"Do you really think he'll show his face?"

"I don't just think, I know. Mom informed me yesterday that she told Dick it's important for family image that he attend. So I am pretty sure we will be your congenial co-hosts for the evening."

"Well shit. You don't need that. I would think he'd be too embarrassed, but you know him better than I do."

"Oh I think that is debatable." A sound best described as a snort escaped my throat. "Anyway, know him or not, I've stopped trying to predict Dick's behavior. But one prediction I will make. I bet every available single woman will be in shark mode, just like they were after Mark Mitchell divorced Betsy. I probably could start a feeding frenzy by hinting that Dick is even richer than they think."

"You go girl!" Lorna exclaimed.

I laughed. Lorna is not the 'you go girl' type.

A loud buzzing sound reminded me that someone was waiting, not terribly patiently it seemed, to be summoned into my happy abode.

"Damn! Hold on. Someone is at the door." I walked the distance from the hall table to the door. Could I be lucky enough to dodge two bullets in one day, or was this going to be another confrontation with a well-meaning but irritating crusader for forgive, forget, and forge ahead. I opened the door a crack.

"Finally! How nice of you to open the door. I thought I might die and decompose out here," Jane announced. "I heard the phone, so I waited a reasonable time before I rang the bell again, but reasonable ran out a while ago. Who is so important that they can't wait to talk long enough for you to answer the door?" She glared toward the receiver.

"Sorry, Jane. It's Lorna. Not her fault," I said, "I forgot about the door. My mind is a little fuzzy,"

Jane followed me into the family room and plopped down onto the sofa. "Your mind is more than a little fuzzy," she said with no pretense of gentleness. "So what's up with Lorna?"

"She called to remind me that it's time to finalize plans for the reunion festivities," I answered.

"Hey, Lorna," I spoke into the phone, "Jane's here. I have to fill her in on my every spoken word as compensation for having made her stand out in the cold for a few minutes. I'll switch to speaker phone so you can hear me grovel."

"A little sarcastic, are we?" Jane removed her sweater, ran her hand through her newly highlighted locks and smiled at me. She faked casual attentiveness, but I could tell she was assessing my emotional state.

"Relax," I assured her, "I'm doing better today. As I told Lorna I am ready to face the reunion festivities with gusto, even with the prospect that slick Dick will grace us with his professorial presence, which as I just told Laura, I am betting he will. Mom thinks he should and in any event, he got a real kick out of sitting at the faculty table at the tenth reunion. Remember how he kept tapping his spoon on the table and saying: 'Behave kids'?"

Jane frowned. "I hope he has enough sense to skip that specific routine," she said.

Lorna's voice floated up from the phone: "Hey, you two, I just had a thought. Why don't I dump the twins with Irving's mom, and come over? That way we can get the party planning out of the way, and the beasties will be guaranteed a cheerier day than if they stay here, since they woke up today with two goals: annoy each other and defy my every word!"

"Sounds good to me," I said. "You up for some serious planning, Jane?"

Jane shook her head emphatically, apparently happy to do anything to keep my mind occupied, so I suggested Lorna hop into her Lincoln Navigator and come over.

Last month Lorna gave in to Irving's pressure to replace her aging but nifty sky blue Miata with a more practical drive-the-kids-to-soccer car. He nixed the idea of having both. Jane was furious. "She should have kept the car," Jane said almost every time she saw Lorna drive up in the monster machine. "If their budget is so damn tight, Irving should give up his golf membership at the club."

"Jeez, Jane, why does it bother you so much?" I asked about the tenth time Jane remarked on the situation.

"You have to ask? Seriously, Bea, do you ever notice guys watching to see who emerges from a Lincoln Navigator? No! But when Lorna drove her Miata, they always watched." She lowered her chin and raised her eyebrows at me.

"And that matters why?" I asked, truly perplexed. "Lorna is happily married. She has two adorable, even if arguably spawned by the devil, twins. Has it ever occurred to you that she might not be interested in attracting attention from strange men?"

"Well if she isn't, she should be," Jane replied. "Married is nice, but it doesn't always last, and if it does not, a woman shouldn't have to go back into the singles market place with the social skills of Edith Bunker."

I absorbed her words. "Is that how you felt when you re-entered the *singles market place*, as you so delicately describe it, Jan? Did you feel like Edith Bunker?"

"Worse. I was Edith's ugly step-sister," she answered, her tone constrained. "After Bart and I got married, I went from barefoot and pregnant to tennis-shoed and matronly. I cut my hair so short it dried before I was out of the shower, and if I remembered to apply lipstick it was a special day. I wore shapeless clothing and didn't concern myself with what kind of shape was beneath the fabric. Bart never seemed to mind; he appeared to be as contented as I was. Only I guess he wasn't." She stood quietly for a moment before she continued. "After the divorce became final, I decided to rejoin the world of single men and women and the entrance was brutal."

The conversation ended with Jane holding both hands in front of her, palms outward, thumbs touching. She lowered her arms abruptly and turned her face away from mine. No further words were spoken.

While we waited I offered to brew a fresh pot of coffee. "Maybe you should use decaffeinated beans," Jane shouted over the noise of the grinder. "I don't want you to start throwing things. You don't have that many dishes left."

I could tell from the grin on her face that she was teasing me, but I couldn't let it go unanswered.

"Just refrain from mentioning Dick's name, or calling Father Tom to report on my behavior, and you'll be safe. Besides, Lorna will be here any minute and she can protect you."

"Lorna couldn't protect a toad. She is the most non-combative person I know. And say what you want, but I did what any true friend would have done. You were going to make a decision you would have regretted."

"Why? Because if I were single I might have to put up with the insufferable dates you tell me about? That is where you misunderstand my future goals." My voice was calm, but I could taste my anger. "I intend to finish my indentured journey of marital securitization, throw a memorable reunion party, and then head off to Las Vegas to do what I should have done instead of calling you when I found the stupid package."

"You mean file for divorce, Bea?"

"Nope. T'is a much more spiteful plan I have." I smiled sweetly.

"I plan to gamble away every frigging cent of Dick's money so that Mercedes can experience Dick as I never did - dirt poor. We'll see just how happy Miss Easy Pants will be to welcome him to her altar of sexual delights when she realizes home sweet home is going to be in a double-wide at a nearby Trailer Park."

It was quite a vision. My muscles relaxed. "Yup, that's my plan. And then just as soon as I have rendered Dickie-boy financially undesirable, I will legally sever all ties to his name. And in lieu of elder-date-hell, I believe I'll join a cult of feminist fanatics and devote my life to some meaningful cause, like compulsory neutering for philanderers."

The expression on Jane's face was priceless. She obviously thought I had strayed over the tracks from Happyville into the scary section of Madtown. It occurred to me that she may be right.

CHAPTER 5

The next morning I finally spoke to Dick, although the past tense of speak is a poor descriptor of our first encounter since the call from his cellular phone after he found his suitcase and gym bag wedged between the steering wheel and seat back. That first confrontation was harsh but restrained. There was bitterness in my voice that reflected the state of my emotions. I asked him who Mercedes was, and he stammered for a bit, offering erroneous bits of information in an attempt to continue the deception. Finally he stopped trying to avoid the truth and confirmed what I already knew.

"May I come home?" he asked at confession's end.

"You have no home," I said and hung up.

This time our interaction was different. Immediately after I learned about Mercedes, coldness set in, quite like the chill of death. In truth, part of me did die. The part that believed in fairy tales and happy endings was gone forever. Then anger and jealousy complicated the mess.

Anger is often described as red hot, and that strikes me as appropriate. It felt hot. It turned undigested food into lava, a corrosive liquid that burned my stomach and traveled mercilessly back up into my throat. But jealousy is referred to as the green-eyed monster. I'll accept the monster part, but I connect green with warmth, and jealousy is cold. I would describe it as the blue-eyed monster and if I drew it, I would show the dark icy waters of the far northern Atlantic. Those were the emotions I carried with me to our first face-to-face meeting in six days.

Dick arrived right after Ben and Kelly got on the school bus. I watched him drive up as the bus pulled away so I could have ignored the doorbell. Instead I opened the front door and walked into the kitchen.

I missed Dick. That sorry truth hit me as soon as I saw his car. I missed him at dinner. I missed the warmth of his body beside me in bed at night. I missed his rational approach to life and his ability to stay calm when I fell apart. Every time I thought about what had happened, I wished I could talk about it with the one person I always turned to with my problems: my best male friend, my soul mate, my husband – the lying, cheating bastard.

"How could you do this to me? How could you do this to your children? What were you thinking?"

I asked those same three questions repeatedly, sometimes in a restrained nice girl voice that mom would approve of, sometimes not. I would move on to other questions, the *who, what, when, and where* questions; but inevitably I would return to my mantra of "How could you?"

Dick was quiet most of the time. I don't know if he was struggling to think of answers, or if he was simply wishing he'd stayed in his car. In any event, the poor guy looked tired. I almost felt sorry for him. Oh hell, I did feel sorry for him. Of course I also felt like hacking him into pieces, stuffing him into the blender, and turning on the crushed ice cycle – sort of Martha Stewart does the wood chipper scene from *Fargo*.

"So are you planning to come to the reunion?" I asked as I nervously pushed the blender to the far corner of the kitchen counter and made a mental note to pick up some St. John's Wort in the morning.

"Am I welcome?"

"The lake house is yours as much as it is mine. At least until my lawyer gets through with you," I added spitefully.

"So we agree that I have a legal right to be at *our* house." He placed a heavy emphasis on the word our. "However, what I asked, Bea, is am I welcome?"

It was a legitimate question, and the answer had many layers. I was ready to explore none of them. Instead I poured coffee into Dick's least favorite coffee mug and handed it to him.

"I won't throw you out. If that isn't answer enough I am sorry, but it is the best I can promise."

"So then, I assume that it's okay with you if I come."

I shrugged. "I suppose it will spoil the evening for some of the guests if you aren't there. I wouldn't be surprised if a betting pool has been established on how long we last without fighting."

"Are we being just a bit paranoid, Bea?"

"If by we, you mean me, I like paranoia better than my old ways – trusting and oblivious to the evil ways of others."

"That's really harsh," he replied. "Neither of us ever meant to hurt you."

"Well then imagine what damage you two lovebirds could have done if you'd put some honest effort into it, Dickie!" I spit out the last word, his note to Mercedes etched onto my brain.

Dick took a step backwards. His face hardened; his eyes narrowed. The tone of his voice, when he finally spoke, was coldly formal. "I never thought you would find out," he said. "I truly did not mean to hurt you."

"What about her? Did she think about the harm that could come from your little escapade?"

"Merci wants what she wants. She doesn't waste a whole lot of time agonizing over other people. She said once when I was feeling guilty, that what you didn't know wouldn't hurt you."

"Well, she was wrong. It hurt more than you will ever know. But enough! Enough! What do you want? Why are you here?"

"I'm here because I never intended for our marriage to end. I came to see if we could put it back together. Can we?" he pleaded. "I want to come home, Bea."

"Why?" I demanded through clenched lips. "There's nothing for you here. You can't want me!" I swallowed and continued, "You're just like that horrible cheating husband in the movie *She's the One!*"

Dick took another step back. His face predicted his words. I'd heard that tone before when what I said escaped his comprehension.

"You are making no sense, Bea! What the hell is up with you? I come here to try and put our marriage back together, and you are babbling on about a stupid movie!"

"I am not babbling! We watched the DVD together a few months ago. Didn't you identify with it when we were watching it?"

I stomped away and poured more coffee. I did not offer him any.

He glared at me. "I do NOT remember the movie," he hissed, "and I still do not know what you are babbling – oh excuse me, I misspeak – I do not know what you are *talking* about."

My tone was calm in response. "I am *talking* about a movie we watched together concerning a man who was having an affair. He refused to have sex with his wife, and when she demanded to know why, he answered: 'How can I go back to driving a Ford now that I've been in a Cadillac?' Only for you it's a Mercedes. Either way, a Ford must be disappointing in comparison."

"Oh, Bea."

Two words. Nothing more. He simply shook his head, turned, and walked out the door without any further explanation.

What exactly did he mean? "Oh, Bea, don't be silly! Mercedes really isn't all that pretty." Or maybe: "Oh, Bea, no one could be as sexy or beautiful as you. I didn't even notice her voluptuous breasts."

Oh what's the point of putting lipstick on a corpse? I know exactly what he meant: "Oh, Bea, you poor broken-down Ford, there is no lie I could invent to convince you that reality is different than it is, so I won't even try."

I called Jane as soon as the door closed behind him. "Dick was here," I said the minute she answered.

I heard her sigh. "Do I hire an attorney or should finding a bail bondsman be my first task?" she asked.

"Neither." I laughed, the tension of Dick's visit broken. "We kept our guns holstered and just exchanged word-fire."

"Ah, but words can be equally deadly."

"True. As can the words that go unsaid," I replied.

"Such as?"

"Mercedes is worthless. I don't love her. I never did. You are all I need. I can't live without you. I could go on and on, Jane. He obviously did not."

"Well did you tell him you need to know about his feelings for her and for you?"

"No, we were too busy taking verbal potshots at each other. He did say that he wants to come back home."

"Interesting. Will you let him?"

"I don't know. Maybe. The kids would be glad to have him here, but then it might just get their hopes up that everything is going to be like it was, and it can't be."

"No, it probably can never be what it was, but perhaps it would be better than the alternative."

"Oh, Jane, I don't know. Half of me doesn't want to ever see him again, and half of me not only wants him back in the house, but back in my bed! What is wrong with me? How can I even think about having sex with him?"

"God, Bea, I don't know. Imagine wanting to have the man you have loved for a quarter century back in your bed. How disgustingly human! If word gets out, you may lose your standing as a living saint."

"So you think I should let him come home then?" I asked, too tired to even attempt a comeback to her sarcastic chiding.

"I say sleep on it, and if you feel even slightly inclined to have him back in the morning, give it a try." There was a pause and I heard ice rattle as she took a drink. "Remember, Beanie, you can always end the relationship after you have given it a second chance, but if you leave now and regret your decision, you may not have another opportunity to try.

Take it from one who knows. Every now and then I wake up at night and wish for my life before the divorce. Bart wasn't perfect, but I loved him, flaws and all, and I wish with all of my heart that I had not given up on us without a fight!"

CHAPTER 6

In my dream I was whirling effortlessly through a crowd with such grace that my feet did not touch the ground. I also laughed a lot, a giddy slightly mad laugh. "I'm peachy keen," I announced as I breezed past each person. "Yep, just peachy keen!"

The phone's piercing clamor brought me crashing to earth.

"Hello," I mumbled in the vicinity of the mouthpiece.

"Hey, Beanie, did I wake you?"

Dick's voice curled around me. I could almost feel the heat from his body. I snuggled further into the covers and decided that Jane was right. I wanted him back in my life and I most definitely wanted him back in my bed. And that was exactly what was on Dick's mind as well.

"What-da-ya say, Bea? Can I come home?"

"I guess," I replied dragging out the s, "but only if you have ended it with Miss Immorality,"

I heard his sigh. "You mean Merci?"

"Is there someone else?"

"There is no one else; and there is no Mercedes. I broke it off completely. I want to come home."

"Then come," I answered. "But, Dick..."

"Yes?"

"Don't ever hurt me again."

I said it calmly, as if the issue involved something less egregious than the ultimate betrayal of a lover's trust. It was said in a 'please don't ever miss dinner again without calling me' tone; and Dick extended his promise in a manner just as matter of fact. Then as if none of the events of the past week had ever occurred, we talked about the things that married couples talk about: what was happening with Ben and Kelly's activities, did the plumber ever show up to fix the leak in the downstairs powder room, did I need him to pick up anything for dinner?

"I could fix Mexican," I offered.

"That would be wonderful, but I don't go to too much trouble," he answered. I could hear animation return to his voice. His happiness was reassuring.

"I don't mind. Ben and Kelly will like it. They will like having you home even more."

I curved into the pillow, lowering my voice as if my lover's ear were next to my mouth. "I will be glad too," I whispered.

"Me too, Bea! Me too. I've missed you. Thank you, sweetheart. Thank you for giving me a second chance. You won't regret it, I promise," he replied in a joyful tone.

I swallowed any remaining fears and repeated my invitation: "Come home then."

"I will. I'll be home for dinner. See you tonight, honey."

"Dick?"

"Yes?"

"Before you hang up, there's one more thing..."

"Sure, Bea. Anything! What is it?"

"All the clothes you have with you. Drop them off at Filbert's Dry Cleaning. Nothing comes back into the house that hasn't been laundered or dry cleaned."

"No problem," he answered.

I heard the click of the receiver. I doubt that it occurred to Dick, but it certainly did to me, that removing Mercedes from his clothing would be the easy part. Removing her from our relationship would be another matter altogether.

CHAPTER 7

If you will excuse me for employing a vastly over-used saying: It never rains but it pours.

Dick's call came at 6:30 Wednesday morning. Between the signing of our peace treaty and the arrival of the school bus, I tossed on an old robe and alternately cajoled and threatened two grumpy children from their beds, into relatively suitable clothing and out the door to the bus stop. When the yellow vehicle from heaven finally departed, I sat down exhausted.

Seven days alone. One hour and fifteen minutes to soak up the realization that I might be part of a couple again, returning to life as God envisioned it when he took one of Adam's ribs and whipped up a companion for the lonely guy. I should have been ecstatic. Unfortunately, I was not entirely certain that I'd made the right choice when I told Dick he could come home. The phone rang.

Seven days alone. One hour and fifteen minutes to soak up the realization that I might be part of a couple again. I lifted my face toward the kitchen ceiling and prayed fervently: Oh, God, please do not let that be Dick. I do appreciate your heavenly intervention aiding us in the repair of our marriage and all –

truly I do – but I just don't think I can be appropriately loving to him right now. So if it is your will, could you make this be an unsolicited salesperson to whom I will be incredibly polite? Thank you. Amen.

I turned in my chair and reached for the phone without getting up. "Hello?"

"Bea? Hi. It's Ted."

Seven days alone. One hour and fifteen minutes to soak up the realization that I might be part of a married couple again. One old boyfriend on the phone. It seems God has a sense of humor.

"Hi to you too," I said. My heart rate increased dramatically. "Long time since we've talked."

"As I remember it, our last conversation was about twenty-four years ago and involved the disturbing news that you had found Mr. Right."

I remembered the phone call well. Ted was so happy when he answered the phone that rainy spring day but the happiness had quickly turned to formality. He wished me well and spoke with dispassionate restraint about appreciating my honesty.

"That call is not one of my favorite memories," I said.

"Nor mine." He paused a moment and continued, "How are you, Bea?"

The chair suddenly seemed less comfortable. "I assume from your tone that you've heard the rumors about me and Mr. Right?" I asked as I shifted my weight.

"Yeah, well nothing much was ever kept private around here; at least not in our old neighborhood. Although I must say things have sure changed from what I remember. Moorestown has become quite the upscale bedroom community."

His voice had the smoldering warmth I remembered. Is his appearance as unchanged as his voice, I thought. I wanted to ask so many questions: Is your hair still dark brown or has it turned gray? Do you have wrinkles? Are you happy? Do you have glasses? Have you ever had a wife, kids, a dog, a mistress?

I took a deep breath and asked about nothing I wanted to know.

"So have you been living in Colorado long?"

"Ever since college. The only real time I've spent here was summer after freshman year, when it seemed as if every time I left the house I ran into you. Thought I might end up blind from the light reflecting off your rather impressive engagement ring." His voice trailed off and for a moment I wondered if he'd hung up.

"What a summer," he finally said. "Anyway, except for a short visit right after each of my folks died, those three months were my last Moorestown days."

"You never talked to me that summer. Not once! I knew you were angry, but I kept hoping that you would eventually say something. I remember a couple of times I started to walk up to you and you turned away. That's why I didn't come to the funeral home when your parents died. I was worried that even after all the years you might not want me there."

"It's just as well you didn't. Dad was only sixty-eight when he had his accident and Mom died less than six months later. Her doctor said the cancer had been there for a while, but I think her body just gave up caring after we lost dad. I had barely begun to heal from losing him when the call came that mom was in intensive care, and she was gone within a week after I got back to Morristown. I would have had a difficult time seeing you without falling apart."

His voice faded in volume. Finally he continued: "As to that summer after freshman year, Bea, I'm a realist; am now – was then. I watched you with Dick. I could see that you were in love with him, so what was the point of talking to you? I wasn't happy for you. I couldn't have claimed that with any credibility. I guess I could have pled my case. I could have told you I'd love you forever, but unless that love was what you desired, and it obviously wasn't, it wasn't much of an offer. So that fall I left for my sophomore year of college and I just never came back."

I couldn't think of an answer.

"But that's all from the distant past, and I'm glad I'm here now," he continued, his tone upbeat.

"I'm glad too," I answered. "Our lake house is a perfect place to party. We had the tenth reunion party there as well, you know." I was surprised by the awkward formality of my words, but Ted did not seem to notice; or if he did, he was too much the gentleman to comment.

"I know. I got the invitation. It sounded like a great party, but I decided there was a reasonable chance I'd make a fool of myself after a couple drinks, so I passed on the opportunity." His tone was jovial, but somehow I doubted that he was joking.

"We missed you, but I guess if you had to choose one reunion to attend, you chose well." I laughed. It sounded hollow to me. I wondered if it did to Ted as well.

"Yes, absolutely a better choice than the tenth," I repeated, "This gathering of Lord of Hosts High's finest graduates promises to be quite an experience. Attendance has increased by about fifteen or twenty people in the last few days. I think they might be hoping that entertainment will feature the McBane family version of the Jerry Springer Show."

"Don't be too quick to judge, Bea. Sure people are talking, you really can't blame them, but I haven't heard anyone sound glad that you are in this mess."

"I'm not sure you would be the person anyone would share that with. But you're probably right. So tell me, why now? Why did you decide to show up for this one?"

Quiet met my question. I could hear music in the background and the sound of a car engine, so I knew we were still connected. I waited.

"Good question," he finally replied. "S'pose I got a hankering to visit the old hometown again. Besides, I have some unfinished business."

"Stuff to do with your mom's estate?"

"Not that kind of business," he replied.

"How mysterious."

When my comment met with silence I offered: "I'm prying. Sorry. Just being nosy, I guess."

More silence.

"Okay," he said finally, "this is going to sound pathetic, and if I had any sense, I'd keep it to myself. But, hey, you and I always were honest with each other, and I have no reason to behave any differently now. So here's the thing: I never let go of what happened between you and me."

"I don't understand," I said.

"Yeah, you and all my friends." He laughed.

"After the summer of the blinding diamond ring, I went back to school and I guess I just kind of shut down emotionally. Academically, I did well; even better in law school. I actually created a bit of a name for myself in the legal community; but I've carried a shield around all these years. I've avoided being hurt so well, that I've wrecked a number of wonderful opportunities to be part of a committed couple."

I heard a horn beep loudly and Ted mumble: "Get over yourself!"

"Everything okay there?" I asked.

"Yeah, I just didn't move quickly enough when the light turned green for the VIP in the Jaguar behind me. Anyway, as I was saying, I was a little hung up over you. Okay, maybe a lot hung up over you." He laughed again. I was starting to enjoy the sound. "So when the invitation to the reunion arrived, I decided that it was time to forgive and forget. My friends all tell me that is an understatement considering it has been almost a quarter of a century since you dumped me, but I guess some of us mend more slowly than others."

I was not surprised by Ted's answer. Now believe me, I took no credit for Ted's feelings. After Dick's escapade, any feelings of sexiness or even of looking attractive were gone; stuffed with the offending underwear into Dick's gym bag. No, Ted's behavior simply fit the boy I remembered. He was a kind and gentle soul, a person who would commit to his friends as well as to his lovers for life.

"So how do you plan to kill the memory?" I asked, smiling into the phone.

"Well, the way I look at it, I've been carrying this image of you in my head for about 24 years, the way you were when I last was with you: sweet, vulnerable and sexy as hell. I figured maybe if I came to the reunion, I'd luck out and discover that you morphed into a grumpy, hard-nosed little old lady who wears those knee-high stockings my Granny wore. I figured one look and I could finally put the fantasy behind me and move on."

I laughed softly at his confession. "So you need a dose of reality, do you?" I asked. "Well, I don't own any knee-highs, but if you could see me now that would kill the fantasy. I'm sitting here in a grubby old bathrobe. My hair looks like a something from the Night of the Living Dead. I haven't slept much for the past five nights, so my eyes are redder than my hair. To finish the vision, I've gained a good twenty pounds since you last saw me, and I've carried and delivered two babies, each of them weighing in well over nine pounds. You don't want to know what that did to my body! So no knee highs, Ted, but one quick glance would put any longings for me behind you with appropriate finality."

"Make some coffee. I'll bring doughnuts." He said and hung up before I could withdraw the unintended invitation.

Now what should I do? Everything I'd said was true. Nothing of the old Bea had survived. One look and Ted would rush out of the house grateful for having been saved from the fate of ever having to look at me across a breakfast table.

No problem then, I simply have to deliver what I promised, a ghastly vision of middle-aged neglect that will remove me from his fantasy life for good. It is best for Ted and best for me. He does not need me cluttering up his brain, and I certainly do not want his unfounded adoration! In fact, the last thing I want in my life is an old boyfriend.

Yes, I thought with smug satisfaction, as I sipped my cold coffee and licked the cinnamon-sugar from my toast, all I have to do is let him see me as I look now and he will leave running. And that is exactly what I will do.

Ten minutes later I had showered and dressed in my sexiest shorts and T-shirt. My hair still looked as if something was nesting in it, so I pulled it back and restrained it with one of Kelly's multi colored scrunchies. It was the hairstyle I'd worn all through high school.

I decided against make-up, and then applied it carefully. A little L'Oreal barely beige foundation to cover my freckles, some blush to create the illusion that I still possessed cheekbones and just a touch of misty-mauve lipstick. The result was better than I hoped.

I finished just as the doorbell rang. Speedy guy, I thought as I walked to the door.

"I didn't have any classes until third period," Dick announced, attempting to move forward.

He shifted a bag from one arm to the other. I stood firmly planted in the middle of the doorframe.

"I stopped at Ralph's and bought all of the ingredients for margaritas to go with tonight's Mexican dinner," he said. "Then I thought I better drop the stuff off, so you wouldn't duplicate my efforts." He smiled. "You look very sexy, by the way."

Seven days alone. Two hours soaking up the realization that I might be part of a couple again. One old boyfriend on the way to my house. One husband arriving, same time, same place. God has a seriously sick sense of humor.

Dick moved toward me. "Can I come in? I smell coffee brewing."

"It's not a good time, Dick."

I could feel my face redden. How could I feel guilty over a cup of coffee with a man I had neither seen nor talked to in years?

"People have been calling about the reunion and stuff, and well, someone is coming over for coffee," I said in explanation.

He backed away and raised his eyebrows. "So people have been calling, and one of those people is joining you for a little pre-reunion celebration. I wouldn't suppose the person is male and named Ted?"

"What makes you ask that?"

"Let's see: Ted's name is on the list; you're doing a better job of blocking my way in than most of my defensive backs; you've got make-up on at 8:30 in the morning; and you are stammering and blushing like a kid caught with her hand in the cookie jar. Other than that, I would say it is just a good guess. So is it Ted?"

"It is but I am not blushing, because there is no reason to blush. For your information, all I intend to share with Ted is a cup of coffee, so don't go judging me by your own low standards of marital behavior!" The last few words came dangerously close to a scream.

"Whoa! Relax, Bea. I have no concerns about you having coffee with Ted. Good lord, I know I can trust you." He smiled serenely and offered up the bag he carried.

He knows he can trust me, I fumed. How gallant. How unemotional. No blue-eyed monster in control of his psyche. He could care less with whom I have coffee or anything else. Bet he wouldn't be so calm and serene if one of Mercedes' old boy friends was about to visit her!

"Fuck you," I thought. "Thanks, honey," I replied sweetly. "See you at dinner."

CHAPTER 8

Dick left with a wave and a smile, his mood far too jovial for my liking. He claims he wants to come home. He says it is over, I thought. But is it? Maybe he is hoping for a better way out from this marriage, a way that doesn't brand him the evil one. What if he set Ted up to visit me so he could photograph us together and use the pictures to divorce me? Worse yet, maybe he'll use the photos to seek custody of Ben and Kelly as well.

Or maybe I am indulging in the type of paranoid behavior that precedes involuntary commitment to the local psych ward, I thought.

I strode back into the house and slammed the door. Forget the conspiracy theory, I told myself. Dick is happy because he feels like the quintessential conquering hero. He has a wanton wench and a spineless wife both willing to welcome him to their proverbial bosoms. All he has to do is decide which lucky contestant gets the prize. Of course he has no concerns!

Maybe I should give him something to worry about. Maybe I should even the score when Ted gets here. Round two: Dick zero-Bea one.

I plopped down into a kitchen chair. How would Ted respond if I made a pass at him? Laughter seemed the most likely response. I can't keep the attention of a man who has pledged to love me for better or worse; what effect would I have on a man who remembers me as a gorgeous teenager? Unless he has retained enough memories of starlit nights and passionate sex in the back of his dad's truck to color his vision, there is no way I'll be able to entice him into my bed once he's seen me.

"No," I sighed and mumbled to myself, "it's more likely that Ted will take one look at me and run in the opposite direction."

I shook my head in disgust. What was wrong with me?

I hurried back upstairs, turned on the shower, and stuck my head under the stream of water. I blindly groped behind me, grabbed a towel and threw it over my head. Muttering words I forbid my kids to use, I rubbed vigorously, removing all make-up along with the water. Finished, I pulled my hair back and fastened it unceremoniously with a plain brown clip. Then I replaced my decidedly skimpy shirt with a nice maidenly blouse.

When the doorbell rang I was ready to behave and dressed to depress. "Hello, Ted," I said in my best Mother Superior voice.

He smiled broadly. "Trying to remind me of the time we went skinny dipping out at the Branson place?"

"Huh?"

He pointed to the front of my blouse. I'd missed a button and several trickles of water were meandering into my bra.

"I just got out of the shower," I replied in as chaste a voice as I could muster. I gave him a decidedly maidenly glare and said, "For heaven's sake, is sex all men ever think about?"

"Can't speak for men in general. As for me, I didn't say anything about sex. I was just reminded by your dripping wet hair of how beautiful you looked that day."

There was no reason to even attempt a reply. Ted's face told me he was enjoying the situation. His smile, while not smug, was definitely relaxed. This was not the boy I'd known. He looked different, stronger, secure in his body. And he had obviously put some work into that body. His stomach muscles were tight under his polo shirt.

"So do I pass inspection?" he asked.

"Oops. Guess I was a little obvious. Sorry."

"Don't be. I've worked hard for that reaction."

"The work paid off."

"Thanks." He punctuated his words with a wide smile.

I waved him into the kitchen. "Sit. I'll pour us some coffee."

"Bea?" He reached out his hand and touched the small of my back. I turned.

"Yes?" I gulped.

"I'm sorry for the crap I said on the phone this morning, for calling Dick Mr. Right and especially for telling you how I felt when I came home that summer. You don't need any of that now. You've got enough to deal with." His eyes pleaded for understanding.

"It's okay, Ted," I said, forcing back the tears. "I knew I hurt you back then, although I never realized how much. I was so young when I made that awful call, but that's not an excuse. I don't even remember what I said, but I know it wasn't what I should have. If I could go back and take away some of that hurt. If I could..."

"Hush. That's all in the past. Don't beat yourself up," he replied quickly,

I looked away. I wasn't certain why exactly, but it was too difficult to face him. I grabbed the decanter and filled two mugs.

"I hope the coffee is okay. It's just Eight O'clock, coffee beans. Nothing fancy."

"It will be delicious, Bea."

He pulled out a chair for me and I smiled up at him as I sat down.

"Gee, Ted, no one does that any more. Did you miss the feminine revolution out there in the wild west?" I teased.

He lowered himself into a chair and took a long sip of coffee. His eyes never left my face. Finally he spoke, "Look, as far as the wounded heart thing goes, it wasn't all that bad after a while. I haven't exactly been in a monastery for the past couple of decades. The initial angst has pretty much evolved into an occasional what-if daydream after I've had a few too many beers. Well, except for one small total disintegration episode when I heard your voice for the first time in twenty-four years."

He could always make me smile. "So tell me about your years outside the monastery," I said.

"Nothing unexpected. I finished college and went on to law school just like I always planned to do. Summers I interned in a couple public defender offices and I really thought that was the way I would go, but it got old fast."

He sat quietly for a moment, both hands cupped around his coffee mug as if enjoying the warmth. Finally he continued: "I'm not a public defender any more. I gave it up about ten years ago and joined a law firm. Now I do pro-bono work a couple of afternoons a week. It lets me pick my non-paying clients in a way I could not as a public servant. I don't have to do nice things for people I would rather give a good swift kick in the ass, and after I've satisfied all of my do-gooder instincts, the income from my day job pays for all the material comforts I could want."

"And do those comforts include any one special?"

"What? You think I have to pay for companionship?" He laughed.

"No, I did not mean that." I laughed with him. It felt good.

"That's nice."

"What is?"

"Hearing you laugh," he said.

I walked to the coffee pot and brought it back to the table with me. As I poured myself a fresh cup, I asked the question that had been on my mind since he arrived. "Are you happy?"

He hesitated but only for a second or two. "Yes, I guess I would say I am happy. I'm not as rich as Dick. Never will be, but I am certainly comfortable and more importantly, I enjoy each day as it comes. Like I always said: You can waste a good life waiting for the blue-light special!"

"Yes! You did always say that! It drove my friends crazy! Sometimes we could have slugged you, because whatever we were whining about was really important to us, and you would sound like one of our parents or maybe like Miss McCratchen. 'Stop whining about what you can't have, girls, and be thankful for what you do have. Why there are children starving...'"

"Okay, okay, I get it," he said, laughing harder now. "Pretty low blow to compare me to McCratchen."

I sipped my coffee. He opened the doughnut box and handed me a Krispy Cream.

"Oh I do love these sinful little creations," I said.

We ate doughnuts, we drank coffee and we talked. I told him about Ben and Kelly, about Jane's return to elder-date-hell, and Lorna's reluctant conversion to Judaism. The coffee got bitter as the time passed but we kept drinking and talking. Finally Ted asked about the subject I knew he would, but in a different way than anyone else had.

"Are you taking care of you?" he asked. "Are you watching out for Bea in this mess Dick's created?"

Everyone else worried about whether I was taking care of my reputation or my children or my financial future or a dozen other things. No one had asked me such a loving question. It gave me comfort and terrified me at the same time. It was one thing to have vengeful thoughts of hopping into bed with another man, and quite another to experience what I was at that moment.

"I'm doing okay," I finally replied. "And, Ted, to be fair to Dick, no one ever creates this kind of mess alone."

"Yeah, I know. I've heard it from other women friends in your predicament. You weren't a perfect wife. You didn't meet his needs. You didn't stay as slim as you should have. The babies changed your figure or your energy or your desire for sex. But whatever specific things are on your own personal list of contributing faults, Bea, I have one thing to say. When a person loves someone, you don't do what he did, no matter what."

"Dick knows that, Ted. He does. He wants to come home. I've told him he can. We had a long talk and he promised he would never hurt me again."

"He better not, Bea. He just damn well better not!" Ted's voice was pleasant, but his eyes told me he meant what he said.

CHAPTER 9

"So, Bea, let me see if I have this straight," Lorna said. "This morning you gave Dick the green light to return home."

"Yes," I acknowledged with little enthusiasm.

"Then within a couple hours Ted called?"

"Yes," I said in a tone that I hoped would discourage Lorna from continuing to ask for confirmation after every sentence.

"So you hear from Ted after a twenty-four year hiatus; and without any trepidation you invite him to breakfast?"

I gave her my best angry eye squint and did not answer.

She smiled and continued unperturbed. "So your reasoning was that he could see that you've aged like the rest of us, and thereby relinquish any vestiges of love he might still feel for you. So far am I accurate?"

I shrugged, as close as I was willing to come to confirming or denying her questions. Lorna handed me a diet coke and settled into the deck chair beside mine. The afternoon sun warmed my skin and lulled me into a much more relaxed state than I had been in when I called her and yelled into the phone: "I need to talk!"

"But before Ted arrived," she continued, "your soon to be no longer estranged husband paid you a surprise visit. Correct?"

"Yes," I answered, hoping to finish the inquisition and move on to receiving empathy. "Dick didn't have class until 10:30 so he bought margarita fixings for dinner, and decided to drop them off at the house."

"Okay, now I hate to sound stupid, Bea, but this is where it gets a bit hard for me to comprehend. You say Dick deduced that ex-boyfriend Ted was on his way for tea and crumpets..."

"Coffee and doughnuts..."

"Yeah, yeah, whatever. What you ate is not the issue. The issue, as I understand it, is that Dick insulted you by *not* assuming something illicit was going to happen between you and Ted." She raised her eyebrows.

I hissed, "Your point?"

"My point, dear Bea, is that nothing inappropriate did happen. So why are you still so damn upset about Dick's comment?"

"Because the stupid shit wasn't jealous; that's why! Not one fucking iota of jealousy! We could have been talking about me receiving a free sample of laundry detergent in the mail, for all the emotion he expended. I was dressed in shorts and a top that didn't even pretend to cover my underwear. I had makeup on, for heaven's sake! Dick could at least have suggested I cover myself up or ditch the lipstick. But I guess he figured it doesn't matter what is covered or uncovered because I can't look good enough to be an enticement."

Lorna took a bite of her tuna fish sandwich and sat there looking at me. I knew whatever came next would be more serious than the banter that preceded it. She was being far too deliberative to suit me. Finally the suspense ended.

"You know, Bea, I hesitate to meddle in decisions concerning your marriage, but you sound way too angry about this whole 'how did Dick respond to Ted's visit thing' to be thinking about reconciliation. Are you sure you want to let him come home right now?"

"Hell, I don't know, Lorna! I do know I'm angry, but even with that, I miss him so much. Isn't that reason enough to work around the anger? Besides when he called this morning, when I heard his voice, I didn't feel mad. I felt like I wished he were right there beside me in bed. I think we hit a bump in the road, a big bump to be sure, but a bump like in all other marriages. The affair is over and I'm healing. Talking to Dick felt almost like old times."

Lorna did not respond. She sat quietly, chewing and staring at her plate.

"And as Jane says," I continued, "almost just may be good enough,"

"Maybe, Bea. Jane could be right, I guess. She certainly has experienced a similar situation, but be careful about rash decisions. I don't think you are as mellow as you think, so your emotions could be harder to handle than you expect. I mean you certainly have over-reacted to Dick's lack of concern about your visit from Ted."

She took another bite of sandwich and chewed slowly, calmly, deliberately, and then she looked at me with what can only be described as a smirk. "You over-reacted unless..." Her voice and eyebrows rose in unison.

"Unless what?" I asked, positive I was not going to like Lorna's answer.

"Unless the reason you don't have anything to feel guilty about is because Ted's visit simply didn't go the way you intended."

There is nothing more annoying than unjust accusation. Well, nothing that is, except being accused with just cause.

I tossed my half eaten sandwich on the plate. "I have no idea what you mean!" I said.

"Bea, get real. You can't lie to me. I know you. I know how you were with Ted. I was practically in the car with you the first time you two had sex!"

"You absolutely were not!"

"Well, okay not in the car," she allowed. "But how long were you home afterwards before I knew? I know when something's up, and something definitely is."

"Nothing is up except your imagination. I wasn't planning to start my day by having sex with Ted. I am still married in case you forgot, and I don't believe in having sex with one person when married to another. I suppose that puts me in a category of Neanderthal spouses, but it is how I feel. It is how I will always feel!"

"Bea, chill! I believe you. So you weren't planning to have sex with Ted, but I still think you were planning something."

"Planning is a distasteful word," I mumbled.

"Well far be it from me to be distasteful. You want a better word? How is hoping, wanting, seeking, desiring, scheming, dreaming? Any of those strike your fancy?"

"Seeking will do. I like that word best."

She smiled. "Seeking what, Bea?"

"I don't know, Lorna. I suppose I was looking for something the moment I reached for lipstick instead of my usual lip-gloss. I guess that's why I felt so guilty when Dick teased me and then so furious when he dismissed the whole idea of my misbehaving."

"Makes sense to me," she said. "You wanted something. You just didn't know what it was."

"In some ways it is as if being dumped releases some sort of male-like urge to mate indiscriminately. You know what I mean, don't you? You've seen it too. The newly divorced woman hanging all over every guy past puberty."

"Yeah, I've seen it. Remember when Harry walked out on Barbara Sue? She didn't even bother with the puberty standard. She had a grand time with Eddie from the car wash." Lorna rolled her eyes and laughed.

I laughed too. "When Eddie's parents found out, it sure ended in a fury. She was lucky she didn't end up in jail."

"Yeah, Barbara Sue never did look before crossing, kind of considered herself entitled to have whatever she wanted. But let's get back to you and Ted. The bible says seek and ye shall find. It seems you sought. What did you find?"

I struggled out of the deck chair, and rubbed the places where the slats had created creases across my arms and legs. It was strangely comforting to be talking of such things with Lorna. Finally I answered, "I found a man with the eyes of a boy I once knew, and a friend in a person who could easily have told me to take a hike."

Lorna got up and followed me into the kitchen. I waved a wine bottle at her and she simply shook her head yes. She would not be detoured from conversation until she was satisfied.

"Was there no physical attraction at all then, no urge to mate indiscriminately?"

"Oh there was physical attraction, undeniably so, right from the moment I opened the kitchen door." I paused a moment, remembering the expression on Ted's face. "See, when Ted arrived I had just finished dunking my head under water."

That got Lorna's attention. I poured two glasses of wine, handed her one and paused. I did not have long to wait.

"You dunked your head under water? Do I want to ask why?"

"Because I didn't want to look like what I must have wanted to look like when I got dressed initially," I said.

"You have such a way with words, Beanie. Have you thought about a career in journalism?"

"Thank you. I owe my finely honed skills to the Lord of Hosts High School Language Arts Department." I laughed but the sound stuck in my throat.

"Do go on," Lorna said.

I sat down at the kitchen table and she followed.

"There isn't that much more to tell," I said. "Before Ted got here, I changed into the nice discreet blouse I'm wearing now."

"Good decision." Lorna nodded her head for emphasis.

"But I missed one button."

"Oh, Bea, how very junior high." She sighed.

"I didn't do it on purpose!"

"Come on...I've taken psychology 101," Lorna said. "If I learned nothing else, I remember that everything is done on purpose. But continue. This is much more interesting than your initial version."

"Well don't get your expectations too high," I told her, "because all that happened was that Ted made some comment about it reminding him of that time we went skinny dipping."

"Definitely a come on!" She laughed, a hardy self-satisfied laugh. "So Ted said that and...?"

"And for a moment, a really short moment, I felt a sexiness I haven't felt in a long time, and I considered dragging him to the nearest bed."

"But you didn't."

"No. I poured coffee instead, and we started to talk. We talked for hours. At some point I realized that I felt something powerful, but nothing that resembled mating madness."

"What do you mean?" she asked.

I considered my words carefully before I spoke. "I felt connected to him in a way that made me feel safe."

"Safe?"

"I know that sounds weird, because when Ted arrived, I admit that some wanton part of me wanted him to take me in his arms, to show me that I could still be desired." I stopped, embarrassed.

"Oh for goodness sakes, Bea, please don't tell me you are feeling guilty for those feelings."

"Okay, I won't tell you."

"Oh, Sweetie, you are so damn old-fashioned! I really do think it is okay to have felt that way. Even frumpy old Father Tom would tell you that fidelity doesn't mean no cravings outside of marriage," she said. "It just means no sampling from a different buffet."

I smiled. "It was an especially tempting buffet."

"I imagine Ted was feeling pretty tempted as well, especially after the junior high blouse trick."

I stuck out my tongue.

"Further proving the junior high theory," she responded. "So once you decided to stick to coffee, what happened?"

"Well, as I said, we talked, and the more we talked, the safer I felt. By the time Ted left, all the inappropriate feelings were gone. He was simply a dear old friend, and I was ready to concentrate on mending my marriage. It seemed almost as if Ted had come back into my life with a purpose, as if he had given me a gift: the courage to try to comprehend what happened between Dick and me. And who knows, if I understand it, maybe Dick and I can make it as right again."

"So the good Father Tom wasn't so far off base when he suggested that you should take your time to think before asking to end your marriage?"

"Oh please," I snapped. "I'm sorry, but anyone who calls that shameless slut a little temptation is off base even if he hits an occasional home run."

Lorna laughed. "You are so benevolent in your criticism."

I simply shrugged in response.

"So tell us, what do you really think about Mercedes?" Lorna used her best Diane Sawyer voice and pretended to hold a microphone up to my face.

I wanted to play along, but my heart was not in the game.

"I think she is not as good as Dick imagines she is, and not as bad as I wish she were," I said quietly. "And I think – no let me rephrase that – I guarantee that if Mercedes sticks her tight little ass into my territory again, all commandments are off."

CHAPTER 10

Have you ever been to a poorly coordinated covered dish dinner: too many oddly concocted salads and mushy green bean casseroles and nothing to really sink your teeth into? That would be a good description of the first McBane dinner as a reestablished family unit. There was ceaseless conversation without communication, and at least on my part, an incongruous mixture of seething anger and Mary, Mother of God.

As we said grace I pushed all thoughts of Mercedes deep into a pit at the center of my being and covered the whole putrid mess with as much ground cover as I could gather. Throughout dinner I focused on the joy of being a family. I smiled. I lavished attention on Dick and the kids.

At one point Ben stabbed his fork into the filling of his taco. "What exactly is in here?" he asked suspiciously. Ben is famous for refusing to eat anything he cannot identify, by brand name if possible.

"La cucaracha. La cucaracha," I sang, laughing as he reacted to the thought of cockroach filled tacos.

At first Ben flashed an annoyed scowl at being the brunt of a joke, but the silliness of my comment prevailed over adolescent angst and soon he was laughing with the rest of us. Then Ben choked and spurted out a mouthful of taco and the comment that sent my own buried garbage shooting right back up to the surface.

"Oh Mom," he gasped between coughing and laughter, "you sound like my Spanish teacher! Maybe she'll give me an A if I tell her my mom speaks Spanish too."

Such a trivial thing, his comment, but it rendered me incapable of enjoying the remainder of the evening, and what it did to the hours after the sun disappeared was worse.

Ben and Kelly were sound asleep by 10:30. Dick turned off the television and poured the last of the margarita mixture into two glasses.

"Let's sit in the swing," he said. It was not an unusual request. We would often sit on the porch in the early evening, rocking gently to and fro as the night skies inked to black. I followed him out of the kitchen as I had done so many times before.

"Dinner was good, Bea."

"Not bad for an Anglo you mean?"

"Don't go there, Bea," he said in a tired voice as we lowered ourselves onto the wooden swing. "Please don't spoil this night. That's all behind us now. At least it can be if you let it."

Dick pulled me toward him, so that my back meshed with his chest. I rested my head against his shoulder, and listened to the cascading songs of the tree frogs as Dick methodically ran his fingertips up and down my arms. I loved that sensation and he knew it. On an especially horny night ten minutes of that alone could qualify as enough foreplay to transport me to a sublimely intense level of excitement.

And after seven long days of celibacy, there was nothing I wanted more than to lose myself in lust. My body craved the release that only sex provides. I wanted passion to explode and its combustion to burn away the past.

Dick's desire matched my own. "Let's go upstairs," he whispered.

And so we went to our bedroom and performed the dance we'd choreographed over the years. Two individuals, each attuned to the other's rhythm, every step occurring in its natural progression. We kissed and caressed and tasted in turn, and when Dick was ready, I curved toward him. The invitation extended and accepted, we came together with an intensity that had not been present since the early days of our courtship. If it were a movie, it would have been the perfect moment for 'they lived happily ever after' to appear on the screen.

But the audience would not know that the performance mocked the truth, for my mind never began the journey my body took. It stayed alert and judgmental.

How could you even think he could want you, it taunted. She is so young, her flesh so perfect. Is he imagining her now? And now? And now?

As my body acquiesced to its own needs, sadness settled in for the night, a sorrow so deep and overwhelming that it terrified me, and I wondered if I would ever know true passion's release again.

"That was nice, Beanie," Dick murmured as he turned away, snuggled his back against mine, and drifted into sleep.

"Yes," I replied softly. "It always was."

CHAPTER 11

When I was twelve, Nana Kelly died. We drove through the night to a small town north of Birmingham, Alabama, and for the next two days sat with her body in the cavernous sitting room at Bonnet's Funeral Home. I remember hating the room with its faded faux-tapestry fabrics and musty air. I recall trying not to look at the casket, surprised that the other mourners seemed delighted to peer into it, sometimes even reaching in to touch Nana's body.

I Shirley Temple smiled at everyone who stopped to pat me on the head and told myself repeatedly that everything would be fine as soon as the funeral ended and we all went home. And indeed it was a relief finally to wake up in my own bed, to dress for school, to walk my dog. The routine felt gloriously familiar, and I quickly replaced memories of crying and strained silences with giggles and laughter.

If I had allowed myself to contemplate the finality of Nana's death, of all that was lost to me forever, I might have sunk into hopelessness. But I did not. As I would do again many times in the future, I packaged the truth, and the emotions that hinged on it, into a carefully constructed box, sealed it tightly, and stored it in my dandy denial vault. Psychologists frown upon such tactics, but it has always worked for me.

And so I began the first morning after Dick's return with a first-class Shirley Temple smile. I smiled at 5:30 a.m., when Dick nudged me in the middle of my back and announced: "Up & at'em, Bea. Early day today. Ben has band practice before school, and I said I'd give him a ride."

"I can take him if you want to sleep a bit longer," I said, one leg already edging out of bed in expectation of his weary thank you. It did not come.

"No, it's okay. I need to get in early this morning anyway. I've got a ton of tests to correct before first period."

"I'll make breakfast then." I flashed him a grin of appreciation for his extremely unusual and, I decided, quite gentlemanly gesture of reconciliation and trooped off to grind the coffee beans.

I smiled as Ben added sugar to his already overly sweet Honey Nut Cheerios, as we searched for the homework he neglected to put in his backpack the night before, and as Dick patted my butt on his way out the door.

By the time Kelly wandered into the kitchen at 6:45 a.m., I had surpassed Shirley's performance in *Little Miss Broadway* and could have passed for a cum laude graduate of clown school.

"You're happy he came home, too, aren't you, mom?" Kelly asked as she watched me whip an egg for her French toast. "We really missed him, didn't we?"

"That we did, sweetie," I replied. "Do you want bacon?"

"Nah," she murmured, shaking her head side to side for emphasis. She squirmed a bit in her chair, a sure-fire sign that she was about to toss me a question I would have trouble answering. I watched her pinch her lips together. Her forehead had more creases than her grandpa Frank's face when umpping a Rotary softball game.

"You okay, Kelly? You look worried or something."

She sighed. I waited at the plate, bat ready. Suspense ended seconds later.

"You aren't going to make daddy leave again, are you?"

Fast pitch, low and outside.

"Oh, Kelly, try not to worry about such things. Your daddy loves you so much. He wants to be here with you always. No one is leaving."

"Not even if he goes out with his girlfriend again?"

Inside pitch. Swung and missed. Stra-ike One!

"He isn't going to do that, Kelly, and you should not trouble yourself with thoughts about it. So, let's decide what movie grandpa and grandma are going to take you to this Saturday while daddy and I are at our reunion party at the lake house."

"Well, okay. But, mommy?"

Pitcher winds up. A quick look to first then lets it rip.

"Yes?"

"Ben told me daddy must like her better than you. Does he, mommy? Does he like her better than you?"

Batter caught looking. Called strike.

"Kelly, honey, that's a tough question." I swallowed. I took a deep breath. I said a prayer without words. "Do you remember last year when Lainey McAllister moved to Moorestown?"

"Yes." Her answer dripped suspicion.

"Do you remember what happened between you and your best friend Susie and how hurt she was?"

"Not fair to bring that up! I didn't mean to hurt Susie."

"I think it is fair, because you asked me a question and the answer is right there in your own head. When Lainey moved here she became the most popular girl in the fourth grade. Everyone wanted to be her friend, to ride ponies at her dad's riding stables, to sail with them on their sailboat. You wanted to; Susie wanted to. But while Lainey thought you were pretty cool, Susie didn't suit her. So for a little while you chose Lainey, and Susie's feelings were hurt. But then you changed your mind. Why?"

"Because I missed Susie."

"And what happened next?"

"I told Susie I was sorry and we were best friends again."

"So there's your answer. Dad said he was sorry and we are going to be best friends again too."

God I'm good! Base hit! Tying run at third and heading for home!

"Well daddy said he never wanted to leave. So you better not make him go away again or I'm going with him!"

Runner out; game over – a heart breaking loss.

"Kelly?"

"What?" She looked at me through sullen eyes.

"You have to understand. I mean it isn't that..." I struggled for a way to explain so that she could comprehend the incomprehensible.

"What do I have to understand?" she whined.

"Nothing. It's time for the bus, silly girl. Don't worry. Everything will all be okay. I promise."

"Mom?"

"Yes?" I held my breath. There was no way I could be up to bat again.

"Daddy drove Ben to school. Would you give me a ride?"

"Sure, baby. Go on out to the car. I'll be right there."

The way I look at it, there are days when you just have to give the fans some special treats.

CHAPTER 12

I clung to my smile all the way to Kelly's school. I knew she didn't mean it when she said she would go with Dick if he left again. Still it hurt, and even worse than how her words made me feel, I knew it was bad for her or for Ben to get caught in the middle of our marital problems.

I decided that I should talk to Dick about what had happened after he left that morning; to make sure he did his part to protect both kids from any unnecessary anxiety. As I watched Kelly run off to join her clique of girlfriends, I glanced at my watch. If I didn't get stuck behind any school buses, I could be at the high school ten minutes before Dick's first period class.

As luck would have it, I had free sailing for the two miles between the schools, and I whipped into the parking lot with plenty of time for a quick conversation. Luck, however, ran out just as I opened my door.

"Beatrice McBane!" Her unmistakable foghorn voice boomed behind me. I turned to face her.

"Hello, dear. How are you?" she asked.

I was just fine until now, I thought. Forget seeing Dick before first period. Mary McCratchen would talk until lunchtime unless

I beat a hasty retreat. Once she began to relate life McCratchen, there was no stopping her. I usually listened with a polite smile on my face, long after everyone else beat a hasty retreat, but that day I opted for rude.

"Sorry to be abrupt, Mary, but I need to talk with Dick before class, so I really have to run."

"Of course, Beatrice, you go right on ahead. I just saw him pull into the parking lot a few minutes ago. He should be in his room by now."

That stopped me in my tracks. "Are you certain it was Dick you saw? I believe he came in much earlier this morning."

"Oh yes. I yelled: 'Hello there, Richard,' and he answered: 'Looks like a fine day.' Then he went on into the building."

"Well, I better do that too," I said.

I found him in the rear of his homeroom, tacking papers to the bulletin board. He looked as handsome as when I'd first met him. His muscles were firm and strong from the conditioning required for any coach who believed in leading by example. It was not too difficult to imagine how Mercedes fell for him, just as I once did.

He turned and looked across the desks to where I was standing.

"Hi there," I said.

"Hey, Beanie, what are you doing here?"

"I need to talk to you."

"What's up?" He looked worried.

"Nothing major. I drove Kelly to school this morning, because she was quite upset at breakfast. Seems you told her you never wanted to leave home, which made me the bad guy in her eyes for making you go away. She's threatening to leave if I do that again. So I came to tell you that we both have to be careful how we talk to the kids about what happened."

"Oh Bea, I am so sorry. I didn't think about how what I said might make you look. I meant to reassure Kelly, not accuse you. I'll be more careful from now on. Sorry. Really."

He did sound incredibly sorry, but I could not seem to smile my forgiveness. Why? What was still bugging me? Oh yes, I thought, that one small detail. "Apology accepted," I said. "But before I leave, Dick, I do have a question."

"Sure, babe, what?" His relaxed smile was enticing.

"Well, you see I ran into Mary McCratchen on my way in and she commented on how you had just arrived. So I am trying to figure out why you were just getting to school minutes ago when you left home more than an hour ago?"

Goodbye smile. Dick visibly stiffened.

"I came here, Madame Inquisitor, immediately after I dropped Ben at school, but a little while ago I realized I hadn't finished my coffee in the rush to get Ben off, so I dashed out to get a Starbucks. Satisfied?"

Let it go, Bea, I thought; but I couldn't. "It just seems strange that you would leave the house so early, which you almost never do. Of course you told me you had tons of papers to correct. What I can't figure out is how did you get them all corrected and still have time to go out for coffee?"

"What is this, Bea, the third degree? What do you imagine I was doing? For god's sake, do you think I dropped Ben at band practice and rushed over to Merci's for a quickie?" His eyes flashed anger. I moved back a step. "I certainly hope that's not what you are implying, because I resent the implication. Is that what you think, Bea? Is that what brought you running over here?"

"No. I honestly came to talk to you about Kelly, but when Mary said you just got here and I knew you should have been here for more than an hour by then, it made me wonder. I'm sorry. I guess I panicked."

"Well you can't panic every time I am off schedule or don't do exactly what I've said I will do, because I can't live that way. I'm back and you have to trust me. I told you the thing with Merci was done, and it is."

The door to the classroom opened a crack. "Okay if I come in, Coach McBane?"

"Sure, Scott, come on in. Bea, I'll see you at home tonight." He turned his back. I was dismissed.

I left the classroom and the building. The good news is that for once I did not immediately call Jane. The bad news is that for once I did not immediately call Jane, because she surely would have stopped me from doing one of the dumber things I've ever done.

I got into my car, smiled my final Shirley Temple clown school smile of the day, and drove out of the faculty parking lot and directly to Casa de Merci.

The building was not what I'd hoped. No plastic flamingos in the front yard. No red lights in the windows. The structure in front of me was just a run of the mill building in an ordinary suburban neighborhood.

It was a painful discovery. I wanted the place where they had been together to look foreign and disreputable. I wanted it to be somewhere Dick did not belong. But it looked normal. The front door was just a door. The building number was not 666 or any other meaningful combination of numbers.

I parked in the rear of the building and sat in the car until my breathing returned to normal and my legs seemed capable of propelling me. Two deep breaths, then I opened the car door and walked into the building and up the steps to the second floor.

There it was: apartment 2-C. How many receipts had I seen with that apartment number on it? Ten? Twenty? I couldn't remember. I pressed the bell and lowered my head so that she would not recognize my face if she used the peephole. Either she did not bother to check, or my subterfuge worked, because the look on her face when she opened the door and was close to true terror.

"What do you want?" she stammered.

"I don't know. I just came. I need to talk."

I could tell the last thing she wanted was to have a conversation with me. It was obvious from the look on her face. Then just when I thought she would slam the door in my face, she surprised me. She shrugged and waved me in. "I have an appointment at 9:30," she said.

"I won't stay long."

I felt incredibly cold. Many times in the past week warmth deserted my body, but never so dramatically as when I walked into that apartment. I looked around. It was an incongruous mixture of feminine decor and furniture obviously chosen and most definitely paid for by a beer and football kind of guy. I saw where Dick would have sat to watch her big screen television. I could picture him with her perched on his lap, the two of them devouring popcorn before starting on each other.

I looked across the living room into the bedroom. I knew what I would see. There in all its decadent majesty stood the four-poster bed Dick once described to me. We had been sitting on the porch swing, and I made some comment about needing new bedroom furniture. Dick said, "Just don't buy a plantation bed. Those posters can make a guy feel insufficient in comparison."

"When have you ever slept in a bed with posters that look like that?" I asked laughing.

"I haven't," he said, laughing back. "But I saw a picture of one in a magazine, and that was intimidating enough."

He paused. "It did look like a bed meant for decadent pleasure, though," he added. "Speaking of which..."

His fingers had stroked my arm. He always did know how to divert my attention. Unfortunately, he wasn't there to divert me that morning.

I turned to face the enemy. She looked chic and confident in a red sleeveless sheath and open-toed sandals with heels higher and thinner than I have ever worn. I slumped into my cotton tee and desperately sucked in my stomach.

"Did you know Dick was married? Did he tell you he had a wife?"

"Yes." She looked at me with undisguised scorn. "He talked about how devoted you are to your kids. Said you are a great mom."

"Oh I see. So did he think we might adopt you?"

She did not seem impressed with my sarcasm. "Is there something you want here?"

"I don't know."

"Well, then if you will excuse me, I have a job interview to get ready for." She walked to the front door and waited for me.

I hated her for her icy composure. I hated her for her contemptuous tone. And damn it all, I hated her for her tiny butt and impressive frontage. I moved toward the door until I stood within a foot of the enemy.

"Sure I'll go," I said. "I wouldn't want to keep you from your job interview, although I'm surprised you plan to work. I thought you just spent your days stealing other women's husbands."

"My job interview is for teaching at a private elementary school," she replied showing no emotion. "As to stealing, I only accepted what was freely offered. Now if you don't mind?"

I searched for something awesome to say. I needed the perfect one-liner, the threat of all threats, the mother of all pronouncements. But nothing clever came to mind.

"Stay away from him," I hissed as I walked past her.

"Or what?"

She shook her head, gave a dismissive wave, and shut the door.

I leaned against the wall outside her apartment. I knew she would be physically attractive, but I had hoped for some minor defect. I found nothing to give me solace. Her body was magnificent, her composure secure. If it came to a battle for Dick's affection, a massacre was inevitable, and she and I both knew who would be standing at the end.

CHAPTER 13

I drove home unaware of where I was going, a swallow returning to Capistrano, a salmon swimming upstream. I have no memory of walking into the house, or of getting into the shower. I must have spent an inordinate amount of time scrubbing the memory of that visit off of my body, however, because when I toweled off, every square inch of the bathroom was dripping from the steam.

I huddled shivering in a chair for nearly an hour before calling Jane and Lorna to pour out the tale of my misadventure, but it took only ten or fifteen minutes until they arrived to tend my wounds. They surveyed the situation quietly, compassionately. One of them wrapped an afghan around my legs. Another placed a mug of hot lemon flavored tea in my hand. I took comfort from their concern, but my voice had slipped back into hiding, tucked somewhere too deep within for me to summon it. I sat silent and unmoving as they hovered over me.

"What was she thinking going there?" Lorna spoke first.

"Who knows," Jane responded. "She has not been rational lately. I just knew something like this was going to happen if we left her alone."

Lorna brushed a stray hair back off of my forehead. "That little bitch had some nerve talking to our Bea that way!

"I'll say she did; damn her! I wish I'd been there. Then we'd see who would be so upset now," Jane replied, her fist clenched in emphasis.

"You know, Jane, for the life of me, I just cannot understand what Dick thought would happen when he started that relationship. And after it began? My god, the little slut's apartment was less than twenty minutes from here! Didn't he think about the consequences if someone saw them together?"

"Duh, Lorna, come on! Do you really believe his brain was the organ controlling his behavior?"

A snort acknowledged Jane's point. "Damn it!" Lorna exclaimed. "Men are pigs!"

Words finally found their way to my mouth. "I can hear the two of you talking, and I'd like to join in, but I can't move. I feel like a very cold, very stupid corpse."

They both jumped at the sound. Lorna leaned forward to hug me in delight. Jane smiled, but her eyes brimmed with tears.

"Well as corpses go, you are poorly prepared for viewing," Jane replied in a light tone as she swiped at her tears with the back of each hand. "That nightgown is remarkably ugly, and your hair seems to have encountered a tornado."

I looked down. I was wearing a threadbare cotton gown, a relic from the days of nighttime feedings. I reached up and felt my hair. "I think I stayed in the shower too long. I don't believe I combed it afterwards. The water was hot. I feel so damn tired."

"It's okay, Beanie. It has a certain streets of London appeal," Lorna murmured, flashing a look of warning at Jane.

Jane sniffed, not the least bit hindered by Lorna. "I presume you mean 'a certain streets of London appeal' as in multi-colored spikes and multiple body piercing? Doesn't sound like Beanie to me."

"Please don't call me Beanie." I whispered. "I don't want to be called that ever again!"

"No problem," Jane replied. "In fact after today's foolishness, I suggest we have a ceremony around the campfire and change your name to *She who forgets to look before she leaps.*"

I kicked off the afghan. Warmth was returning to my body, internal lava its source. "Very funny," I said, "but I'm serious. I don't want a nickname that points out that I don't! Women are defined by their breasts and mine are deficient!"

"Sweetie, you're serious, aren't you?" Lorna finished folding the discarded afghan and sat down beside me on the sofa. Her arm rested on my shoulder.

"Oh I am serious all right. I saw her. I saw how she looks. I have never looked that sexy! Never! No wonder he wanted her. I don't fit the standard for sexiness. Mercedes does, but not me." My voice trailed off.

"There is no standard for sexiness," Jane answered, her voice un-Jane-like in its gentleness.

"Wrong!" I shrieked. "There is a standard. The standard is perfect breasts!"

"You really believe this, don't you, Bea."

I had heard Lorna use that same tone with the twins when they freaked out at the sight of a buzzing insect or green vegetable. She stole a quick glance at Jane and then flashed me her best 'mom is here now, so everything will be okay' face.

"Yes!" I yelled. "It's not just what I saw today. I mean think of every movie you've seen in the past two or three years. No matter what the plot, no matter how flaccid-faced or paunchy the male lead, his co-star will be young and beautiful, and her perfect breasts will be flashed across the screen at least once before the movie ends!"

I could hear my voice rise in pitch. I struggled to speak in a more controlled tone. "I hate being flat-chested! If I had nicer breasts, Dick wouldn't have left me."

"Oh, Bea, that's not true." Jane sat on the arm of the couch and patted me on the hand.

"No, Jane, Bea is right," Lorna said. "Although not about Dick needing to get his pleasure elsewhere because of her breast size. He was just being a shit."

She looked directly at me. "You're a beautiful woman, Bea, but it is true what you say about films, and about how they make us feel. And I for one do not remember seeing even one penis in all those films."

"You have a point there. Pun intended," Jane said. "A couple can be going at it and the woman will be totally naked and her partner will look like he's dressed for casual day at the office. Oh sure, you might see a naked back, his stomach, even an ass now and then, but his penis will remain discretely tucked out of view."

She met our stares. "Don't give me those looks. I've watched a film or two on cable for inspiration, and there is a definite inequity."

"Exactly," I said, fighting to keep the laughter out my voice at the thought of Jane watching porn. "Every film has bare or barely-covered breasts; perfect little mountains of joy! So women leave the theater feeling as if we do not quite make the cut, while the men leave satisfied with themselves no matter how insufficient the penis is that's tucked behind their zippers."

"Someone should do something," Lorna declared, a slight upward turn to her mouth betraying her own attempt at a serious tone. "We could start a national organization that demands equality in films: at least one penis per every two breasts displayed on screen."

"We could sell bumper stickers: SHOW US YOUR PENIS," Jane chimed in.

"Or better yet: WE LIED – SIZE MATTERS!" Lorna said with a giggle.

Jane took the mug out of my hand and refilled it before offering it back. "Drink up, girl. We have miles to go and penises to expose before we sleep."

By now all three of us were laughing. "I don't know what I would do without you," I said reaching up to hug both of them.

"You don't ever have to do without us." Jane said, returning my hug.

We hugged and then we sat in silence, Lorna on one side of me, Jane the other.

Lorna finally broke the silence. "I hate to ruin the mood," she said, "but unless you are going to cancel, and I would not blame you if you did, we probably should talk a bit more about preparations for the reunion."

"I don't want to cancel," I said. "Actually we're in pretty good shape. The caterers are all set. Tomorrow I thought I'd drive out to the lake and decorate while the kids are in school. Want to come?"

"I certainly do," Jane said. "I want to help, and I feel a need to keep you on a very short leash until you show better judgment about whither thou wanders."

Lorna shook her head in agreement.

The phone rang.

"Shall I get that?" Lorna asked.

"Oh yes, please. If it's my mom she'll instinctively feel my angst and will be all over what she calls my negative outlook, and I could do without a lecture. Tell her I'm up to my elbows in meat loaf mix, and I'll call her later."

I listened as Lorna answered and chatted. It obviously was not mom, because Lorna was asking too many questions about how the person had spent the last twenty years. Just before she hung up she said, "Want to join us at the lake house tomorrow? We are going to decorate. Seriously, I know she will love to have you there. Absolutely! Let me ask." She lowered the receiver and called across the room, "What time will we plan to get there, Bea?"

I shook my head back and forth vigorously. "I would rather it were just us three," I whispered.

"Bea says ten o'clock, Ted. See you there. Bye."

Ted? She was talking to Ted? I could not believe it! Lorna had just invited Ted to the lake house. She knew how I reacted to him when we last were together. Magnificent Mercedes was obstacle enough. I did not need Ted interfering with my reconciliation with Dick.

I turned, grimaced at Jane, and waved my arm in exasperation at Lorna. Jane frowned as well, obviously as upset with Lorna as I was.

"Look you two," she said. "I'm already late for my dentist appointment, so I'll make this quick. I want to say something about what Lorna just did, and I hope my words are not taken wrong, because I don't mean any disrespect."

I eagerly awaited her pronouncement.

"Bea, I am glad Lorna asked Ted to come along."

Glad? I did not ask for glad! "You are what?" I cried out, disappointment dripping from each word. "Come on, Jane! How can you be glad for God's sake?"

"Easy. The four of us had fun times together in high school, and you are in serious need of some fun right now. And, Bea, I mean no disrespect, but you have not been taking care of yourself since this whole mess began. For one thing, your hair is beyond awful. Go to the salon this afternoon, and please throw that horrid excuse for nightwear away."

Lorna gave a quick almost imperceptible nod of agreement, walked over and stood in front of me. She put one hand on each of my shoulders and said, "Bea, I'll pick you up at eight-thirty tomorrow morning. Jane is right; spending a little time with Ted won't hurt you. He always could make you laugh. Just for one day we are going to pretend we are all back in high school, that you never met Dick, and that none of the bad stuff ever happened. Let's be the three bears and our hired woodsman for the day. Okay?"

"I don't know," I said. "I like the idea of a three bears day, although not the woodsman part. But even so, I could certainly use some laughter."

"So it's a date?"

"Yeah, it's a date, but I've gotta tell ya, I certainly hope I don't find a certain dark-haired Goldilocks sleeping in my bed when I return."

CHAPTER 14

I'm sure you've heard the adage: You can't go home again. Let me add to that piece of folk wisdom. You can't go back to the lake house either.

The morning began pleasantly enough. Lorna arrived promptly at 8:30 AM. We picked Jane up and talked non-stop throughout the one-hour drive. No one mentioned Mercedes or any other depressing subjects. Even my hair got rave reviews.

"It's a bit shorter, isn't it," Jane asked, "and the color is different too. I like it."

"Thanks. After you two finished your less-than-kind critique of my tresses, I called Mary Sue and she fit me in between a couple other clients. Said she couldn't let me go around looking like a 'poorly prepared corpse.' I just intended to have her cut about an inch from the ends but she talked me into covering the grey and even adding a few highlights. Cost a bundle, but I figured a twenty-fifth reunion is a time to splurge."

"You will be the hit of the evening."

I laughed. "Woulda been anyway. Perhaps for a different reason."

"For sure, Ms. Notorious," Jane said, "but the rest of us better get busy if we want to get noticed for any reason."

"You are so right," Lorna said. "Not only do I still have to do something with my hair, I haven't even found an outfit yet. What are you two wearing?"

"Don't know," I said. "If the weather service is correct, it is going to be hot even after the sun goes down. So I'm thinking shorts and a nice top, or maybe a cotton dress."

"You have the legs for shorts." Jane said. "I wouldn't be caught dead in anything that ended above mid-calf."

"My legs are too heavy for shorts," Lorna said. "Oh let's face it; I'm too heavy all over. Maybe the tent company can just drop something extra off for me to wear. Women should not have babies in their thirties. I gained sixty pounds the day I conceived, lost two pounds per twin delivered, and nothing has sprung back in the six years since."

I leaned forward from the back seat and patted her on the shoulder. "Oh for heaven sakes, Lorna, you don't weigh more than 20 pounds over your high school weight. You look just fine in shorts, but if it would make you feel more comfortable we can all wear long skirts," I said.

"How about we cover even more by layering with matching trench coats?" Jane added.

"Not a chance!" Lorna said in her best Moorestown Pep Squad voice. "Alice McDermott is coming to the reunion, and the little creep was always stealing my dates. I think I just might wear a nude latex body girdle under a slinky dress, and sashay my stuff right past her husband."

"You mean Larry the Letch?" Jane asked. "You don't have to do anything that obvious. If you don't knee Larry in the crotch when he leans into you, he thinks you're hot for him. I hear Alice has installed an invisible fence in hopes of keeping him home at night."

We laughed away the final miles of the trip, and probably would have continued laughing till the day ended if Lorna hadn't complicated everything with Ted's presence.

A decadent red convertible was parked in the driveway.

"Wow," Lorna said. "Irving said Ted was at the dealer picking up his new car. Apparently Ted needed to replace a car that had driven its last highway and was ready for the junkyard. He found one he loved, and thought this was the perfect time to spring for it, so he could drive it back to Colorado."

"Wow is right. This doesn't look like something the Ted I remember would own. Very sexy!" Jane added as she circled the car.

"Sexy is an understatement! No wonder Irving looked so smug. He had said Ted's only decision was color; that the dealer had two ready to drive off the lot, one in red metallic and the other in polar silver metallic. I figured he was buying some kind of truck-sized SUV for the hills of Colorado, so I think I shrugged and said something like *whatever*."

"Well, this is no truck, and I don't know how silver looked but this color screams sexy owner," Lorna said, running her hand over the leather headrest on the passenger seat.

"Oh for heaven's sake! The shower is upstairs if either of you need to cool off," I said. "I am going to start carrying boxes out to the back yard. Why don't the two of you go reintroduce yourselves to Ted? He must be around here somewhere, probably fighting off other middle-aged groupies."

Neither argued with me, and I must have made ten trips between the car and the yard before anyone came to find me.

"Need help, Bea?" I did not have to turn around to know who belonged to the voice.

"Oh sure wait until the last load to come out." I handed him the box I pulled out of the trunk. "Have Lorna and Jane stopped drooling over your car yet?"

"I think they are nearly finished." He laughed. "You know, Bea, this is kinda déjà vu. You used to get rather huffy when Lorna and Jean flirted too much with me."

"Don't be ridiculous!" I turned my back to him and searched carefully for any items that might be hiding in the trunk. "In case you forget, I'm married; so it is of little concern to me who flirts with you. I just thought the two of them should be a bit more helpful with lugging everything out to the back."

"It's incredible."

"What's incredible?"

"The way your eyes change color when you're angry."

He stood there holding that damn box and looking at ease with himself. I on the other hand was feeling anything but comfortable.

"I can't do this, Ted."

"Can't do what, Bea?"

"I can't pretend everything is fine and dandy. I can't do small talk. I can't flirt."

"Hey, calm down, sweet girl."

I flashed him a warning look.

"Sorry, I know I shouldn't have called you that. But you are sweet. Anyway, you are here with three people who love you, Bea. Just good clean best friend forever love. Nobody is asking you to do anything that makes you uncomfortable. We're just trying to make up for the fact that you've had to deal with some stuff you didn't deserve."

I opened my mouth. He cut me off before the words emerged. "Don't start with the two sides to every story crap. You know how I feel about that. You don't have to make small talk or flirt, and I promise I'll behave."

"You promise?"

"Absolutely. So give it a try, Bea. Just relax and enjoy the afternoon. We'll make this place look festive. Lorna tells me the three of you bought every strand of colored lights and outdoor decoration you could find."

I nodded and offered up a hint of a smile.

"Good. I am hereby offered up then as your official fetch and handy man for the day."

I watched him walk toward the back yard. Lorna and Jane appeared, dragging a table toward the lake, and he yelled that he would help them. With a sigh, I followed.

Physical labor is a wonderful elixir. The three bears and the big bad handyman worked for hours to turn the lake house into a veritable wonderland, and slowly but surely, I relaxed and eased myself into the afternoon. We could not, as Lorna had hoped, pretend we were all back in high school, that I never met Dick, and that none of the bad stuff ever happened, but we did find solace in hard work and companionship. And given the circumstances, I considered that a pretty good result.

CHAPTER 15

The morning of the reunion dawned bright and humid. I climbed out of bed and pulled my nightgown over my head, a properly sexy silk nightgown, pale apricot, knee length with a deep cut V-neck and barely over the shoulder sleeves. My outfit did not affect my mood. All my old cotton sleepwear had been transported to the Goodwill box shortly after Lorna and Jane left the house on Thursday, otherwise I would have chosen the ugliest among them.

Dick rolled over and pulled my naked body back onto the bed. "The silk thing was nice, but this, Bea, is my idea of sexy sleepwear," he said.

I did not answer. His words from the evening before still stung. My icy response appeared to break through his oblivion.

"Look, Bea, I'm sorry I was so angry with you last night," he said. "I shouldn't have yelled at you. I don't know why I did."

"Perhaps because I upset your little friend and you were feeling protective of her."

"You're wrong, Bea. Merci is not my concern. The problem is how your behavior affects us. She is a bad chapter in an otherwise good book. But if you insist on re-reading that one lousy chapter, you will destroy us." He began to run his fingers up and down the arm closest to him, an invitation to stop talking.

I shrugged off his fingers. "She didn't have any trouble finding a way to leave that one lousy chapter so she could tell you about my visit."

"She called me at school, Bea." Exasperation dripped from his voice. "It was a quick call. Two minutes, maybe three. She simply asked that I do what I can to keep you from going there again. She really felt threatened by you."

"Threatened? By me? You gotta be kidding!" I snorted my distain for the concept.

"No, Bea, I am not. She was distraught. She barely got herself pulled back together in time for her interview."

I could not believe what I was hearing. I had seen Mercedes, had listened to her condescending compliments about my mothering and her harsh command to get out of her apartment. There were no signs of fear, no tears, no discomfort. Obviously, however, she knew what to say to Dick to turn the situation to her advantage.

"She seemed just fine when I left."

"Well she wasn't," he answered. "But my concern, as I've repeatedly said, is not her but us. We need to move past this. Can you do that, Bea?"

"I'm trying."

"That's my girl." He leaned over and nuzzled my neck.

"You didn't go to see Mercedes Thursday morning then?"

"I told you no, didn't I?" There was no mistaking the irritation in his voice. I doubted the nuzzling would continue unless I gave up my quest. I could not.

"You did not say no. You said I was wrong if I thought you went there for a quickie. So do you mean you did not go there at all, or do you mean it was not quick?"

"Oh for heaven's sake, Bea!" He turned his face from me and got out of bed. "It is far too early for semantics. Believe what you want. No matter what I say, you will anyway."

I heard the bathroom door slam and the shower begin. What was wrong with me? All those days in church chanting prayers about forgiveness and here I was unable to accept a sincere apology from the man I love. I quickly dressed and left the room.

Breakfast was Ozzie and Harriet revisited. Guilt is a wonderful motivator. I made pancakes from scratch. I heated the syrup and pan-fried the little sausages Ben likes. I even dug out the pineapple shaped place mats Dick's mom brought us from Hawaii and added cloth napkins for effect.

"Wow, mom," Kelly exclaimed when she saw the table. "It looks like a party."

"I thought a party might be a nice way to start the weekend," I replied.

My efforts seemed to pay off. Everyone exclaimed that the pancakes were superb. Ben ate six sausages along with his share of pancakes and Dick teased that he must have an extra stomach somewhere to hold all food. After the kids finished their breakfast we had our second cup of coffee sitting on the swing. I commented on how nice the flowers looked so early in the season. Dick said he should dig out his records to see whether any of the cars needed to be serviced. I offered to check for him on Monday. He replied that I would be exhausted from cleaning up after the party and did not need an extra task. Polite would have been an understatement if used to describe our conversation.

Before Dick left to drive Ben and Kelly to my parents' house for the weekend, I handed him a list. "There are still quite a few things left to be done before the hordes arrive tonight," I said. "I have to buy more paper goods because the rental company brought smaller tables than I ordered. Do you mind picking up all the soda and hard stuff?"

"No," he replied, his face unreadable as he scanned the piece of paper.

"And I thought we should both try to be at the lake house by one or two in case there are deliveries or anything unexpected happens that needs our attention. Does that work for you? Should we meet there or here at noon and drive together?"

"The timing works fine, Bea," he replied in a weary tone. "But we better take two cars given the amount of liquor and soft drinks you have me buying. So how about we just meet out at the lake house?"

"Okay," I answered. "Sure. See you there between one and two."

"Right. And Bea, please try not to panic and imagine all sorts of things if I'm five minutes late."

Before I could answer, footsteps thundered down the stairs and Ben and Kelly dumped their suitcases on the kitchen floor.

"Got everything packed?" Dick asked.

Both nodded. "Then kiss your mom and pick up your gear cause over the river and through the woods to Grandma's house we go..."

Ben rolled his eyes in disgust but Kelly giggled. "Oh dad, they only live across town."

"We'll pick you two up late Sunday afternoon," I said. "Be good for Nana and Grandpa. I love you."

"Love you too, mom," they yelled in unison as they dashed out the door.

"See you later, Dick. I love you," I called. He did not answer.

CHAPTER 16

The day flew by. Even with caterers, preparing for a party of almost one-hundred guests is daunting. I checked everything one final time before allowing myself a long soak in the tub.

The water swirled deliciously hot as I climbed in. I inhaled the scent of my Boucheron Bath Gel wafting up from the water, turned the whirlpool jets on high, and sank as low as I could in the water without wetting my hair.

"You look relaxed," Dick said.

I opened my eyes. "Relaxed may not be the best word to use considering that we are about to entertain a hundred people, many of whom we have not seen for fifteen years, and some for even longer than that. I was actually lying here wondering exactly why we are doing this."

"Because we have the perfect location for a party," Dick said, his voice confident and soothing. "Last time everyone had an absolute ball. Remember?" He sat down on the edge of the tub. "Lean forward," he commanded.

"That was a good party," I agreed. "There must have been fifty people who stayed right through to breakfast. I've stocked up on bagels, muffins and orange juice just in case that happens again. Of course if no one stays we'll have to take it all to the shelter tomorrow afternoon. Oh that does feel good," I added as he scrubbed my back with the sponge.

"Bea, I really am sorry about losing my temper yesterday. The answer to your question is a straightforward no. I did not go to Merci's apartment that morning. I'm done with that. She is history. I need you to believe me, and I need you to act as if you do."

"I believe you, Dick. I do," I said. "And I'll stop acting however it was I was acting."

"Like an inquisitor."

I laughed. "Okay, I'll stop acting like an inquisitor."

"Like an over-zealous inquisitor."

Î laughed again. "Maybe a smidgeon over-zealous."

"Like an over-zealous inquisitor from the French Inquisition."

"Don't push your luck." I flicked a few suds at him. "We better get ready. I bet Mary McCratchen is on her way. Sure am glad I don't have to sit with her at the faculty table."

"Don't remind me. Did you know that the class of 1962 had their graduation ceremonies canceled because of a riotous beer party the night before graduation was scheduled? I learned that last month at a faculty meeting. So many fascinating facts, so little time for Mary to babble on and on and on about them."

"Go shower, poor boy. I better get myself dressed and ready for action."

I left him singing in the shower, and found myself humming as well. It felt so good to be reconciled. What a wonderful verb: to reconcile, to bring into consonance or accord.

Some of our guests may be disappointed, I thought. Should be interesting to see if any of them leave early when they realize true love has returned to the McBane household.

CHAPTER 17

All agreed the tenth reunion had been a blast, and as nearly every guest I talked with told me, the twenty-fifth promised to be even more memorable. I felt a twinge of guilt for my low expectations of how my high school buddies would react to our reconciliation. No one appeared disappointed that Dick and I were still attached at the hipbone. In fact there was a palpable sense of relief, as if our happily-ever-after ending lent an extra special aura to the festivities. When Dick and I danced, my arms around his neck and his around my waist, I sighed, confident that my world had righted itself.

I was wrong.

The evening took a definite turn for the worse at approximately 11:45 PM. I'd needed to go to the bathroom for at least an hour, but the band was so damn good that I kept dancing. Finally I decided that I was dangerously close to wetting myself, so I slipped back through the patio doors into the house.

Both bathrooms on the first floor were occupied. I had predicted that an open bar would be a poor choice with this group of hardy drinkers, and judging by the sounds of recycled booze streaming into the toilet bowls – and probably all over the floor as well – I was right.

I headed upstairs. I had shut all doors to the second floor bedrooms in hopes of discouraging trips to their bathrooms. I hurried into the master bedroom, closed the bedroom door behind me, dashed to the bathroom and managed to lower myself onto a gloriously pee-free toilet seat before my bladder's holding ability gave out. I sighed contentedly. All liquid relinquished, I breathed in contentedly and leaned forward, my arms resting on my thighs and exhaled.

The glow of the colored bulbs from the yard below lent a magical touch to the walls in the otherwise dark bathroom. As alcohol from several margaritas flowed through my veins, I contemplated whether anyone would mind if I just took a short nap, or for that matter whether anyone in the overly-imbibed crowd would even notice my absence. I closed my eyes and fell, if not technically asleep, at least into a state of abstract peacefulness. Sadly, peace lasted only a few short moments.

I did not hear the bedroom door open. The first indication I had that I was not alone in my compromising position was when I heard a male voice whisper, "Can you hear me? I don't dare talk any louder than this."

I was torn with indecision. I felt compelled as a hostess-extraordinaire to answer whoever was calling to me in that restrained voice, but I was sitting on a toilet, my shorts and underwear on the floor around my ankles. I decided that covering my naked ass took precedence over politeness; so I quietly reached down and began to pull both panties and shorts upward. Then I heard the next sentence, and understood that the voice was speaking not to me, but into a phone.

"Merci, I'm sorry," hissed a voice I now knew to be Dick's. "Try to calm down. I know I promised to see you before the party, but Bea asked me to run some last minute errands and if I didn't get them all accomplished, she would have been suspicious. She has finally stopped asking about you every day. I don't want to risk making her suspicious again."

I stopped tugging on the shorts and lowered myself back onto the seat.

"I've missed you too," he continued, his voice morphing into a soothing lover's croon. "Look, I will be there tomorrow if I can find an excuse to drive back to Moorestown before Bea, but if I don't show up, you have to deal with it. I told you from the beginning that I would do whatever necessary to protect my children. Stop saying that. You know I care. I don't know what you expect me to do. If Ben and Kelly weren't so damn young, if they were at least both in high school, things could be different, but things are the way they are, and all the tears and threats in the world won't make them any different."

I swallowed repeatedly. There seemed to be no oxygen in the room. For a minute or two I focused on breathing in and out, out and in. Finally I decided that my body could continue to perform the task itself or not as it saw fit. Frankly, I did not care which, and the next few minutes passed without purposeful thought or movement. If Dick told Mercedes goodbye, I did not hear it. Nor did I hear him leave the room. I simply sat there and absorbed the terrible truth. That about which I had obsessed for days and which I had just finally relinquished was true.

All the sweet talk, all the attentiveness was distraction. He had decided to stay in the marriage until Ben and Kelly were old enough to deal with divorce. His desire to come home had nothing to do with love for me. I am a broken down old Ford and Mercedes has won the race.

I tried to identify what I was feeling. Anger? Distress? Bitterness? What? What was it? Why could I not name the emotion? I struggled to know. I had to know. Finally it came to me. Tired. That is what I feel, I decided. Just plain old tired.

I rose from the throne and pulled up my royal garments. Then I turned on the light and took a long hard look in the mirror. There it was, the face of an almost forty-three-year-old woman. Not so bad, all things considered. Freckles here and there, but good clear skin tone. Eyes still acceptable; no major wrinkles; no droopy eyelids. I pushed upwards against the skin on each side of my face. Improvement was possible, but a face-lift was still a decade or so away. I brushed back a few errant strands of hair that had escaped my attempt at a French braid.

Slowly but with a sense of purpose, my energy returned. I pulled off the scrunchie that was holding the braid in place. Sexy color, I thought, even if it is chemically altered. I ran my fingers through the front and shook my head to loosen the rest. I decided I looked a little unkempt, but then so did most of the partying crowd.

With a deep sigh I nodded toward my reflection and straightened my shoulders. Then I pulled up my shirt and removed my bra. "Well, girls," I whispered, looking downward, "you aren't much, but I'm counting on you tonight. Prepare yourselves for battle. If Dick can dance the marital two-step, so can I."

CHAPTER 18

I did not know exactly what I was going to do when I sauntered back out onto the patio, but there was no doubt that it involved Ted. I scanned the crowd. There he was sitting alone on the dock. I grabbed two beers, a decision I was sure I would regret in the morning, although I guessed that any regret related to mixing types of alcoholic drinks consumed, would be lost in rounding if I continued down the path I'd just chosen.

"Hey, stranger," I said when I reached him. "Can I buy you a beer?"

Ted did not answer; just held up his hand and accepted the Heineken.

"Mind if I join you?" I asked.

"I'd love company. Sit." He patted the deck beside him then held up a hand for support.

I slipped off my sandals and dangled my feet into the lake. "Ah, the water feels good," I said.

He allowed himself a quick glance sideways.

"You don't look like you feel so good, though," he said.

"Good observation. Actually I feel fairly awful. I just overheard a Dick and Mercedes conversation."

"Damn it!" He reached over and touched my shoulder. "People shouldn't talk about a subject that doesn't concern them. Try to ignore them if you can."

"Oh much worse than that, Ted. Not people talking *about* Mercedes and Dick; talk *between* Mercedes and Dick." I waited for my sentence to sink in before I added, "He was on the phone with her."

"Ah. I see. That is a bit harder to ignore."

"Yeah, that's an understatement."

"Are you upset about what was said or simply mad that he was talking to her?" he asked.

"Both. Dick promised me that it was over with her. That was our agreement. He could come home, but not if he was still seeing her."

"And you think he still is?"

"No doubt about it. From what he said they were supposed to have had a little roll in the hay this morning but I made his list of things to do for the party too long. So now he has the challenging task of thinking up a reason to drive back to Moorestown before I do. I guess instead of Sunday in the Park, Dick is hoping for a fun day with the tart."

"Jeez, Bea," he asked, "how can you make jokes about it?"

"I don't know. I guess that is how I handle things. Feel bad; tell a joke. Feel worse, tell two jokes."

"Yeah, I guess that is how you've always handled things that were upsetting. Tell you what: this dock is awfully hard. How about we find somewhere more comfortable to sit?"

"How about in your car?" I amazed myself with that suggestion. I could not tell if Ted was surprised as well. His face was hidden from view as he hoisted himself up.

"Your car is a hit with just about everyone," I said in as lighthearted a tone as I could manage. "Some people think it doesn't quite fit your image as sedate old Ted."

When he did not answer immediately, I added: "We don't have to if you'd rather not."

"Sitting in the car is fine with me, but it's kind of tight quarters. Sure you don't mind the closeness?" The question was posed in a casual tone. The look on his face was not.

"Closeness can be good," I said, managing an eight note range, low to high, as I spoke.

Closeness can be good? Great. My voice had the lilt of a preadolescent boy, and my words were inane. Was I always this clumsy at small talk, or is there a preservation of the species gene that makes drivel sound better when we are younger? Will it get easier if I keep at it, or is there an age after which dating just doesn't work without earplugs?

"Bea?"

"Yes?"

"Where did you go? I see you standing there, but I don't think you are actually here."

"I wasn't. I'm back."

"Well, welcome back."

I laughed.

"The car is out front. Do you still want to go, or would you rather just stay here?"

"Actually I'd like to get away from here. Do you think we could go for a short drive? Are you sober enough?"

"I'm quite sober. You, however, are obviously a couple margaritas past your limit. Which limit, if memory serves me correctly, is two."

"I'm a little drunk," I admitted. "But I'm not asking to drive, so it should not be a problem. I really would like to get away from here for a while though. Do you mind?"

"Absolutely not. Your carriage awaits, my lady. And Bea..." He paused.

"Yes?"

"For the record, I never mind doing anything that pleases you."

I followed Ted, and several pairs of eyes followed our departure. I wondered if Dick's were among them, and if he would even give a damn. It was hard not to look behind me to see if he was watching.

"It's beautiful," I said when we reached the car. I looked inside. "You're right about there not being a lot of room though."

"Enough room for two." He reached over and rubbed the tip of my nose with his thumb. My entire body reacted. Who knew the tip of a nose could feel such pleasure?

"You've had a nasty couple of weeks, kiddo," he said as he reached over and opened the car door open.

I climbed in as gracefully as the margaritas would permit, and he waited until I was settled in my seat to carefully shut the door. I could get used to this, I thought.

"There is a full moon out tonight," he said as he got into the driver's seat. "I bet we could see all the way across the lake to your backyard if we drove over to the Branson property."

The Branson property stretched for mile after deserted mile along the lake, and was the rumored location for many a sexual conquest for the Lord of Hosts High School Class of 1988. It was a stupid place to go, a place that screamed illicit sexual activity, an absurdly obvious statement of my un-wifely intentions. The only answer is no.

"Sounds perfect," I said.

Ted started the motor and maneuvered the car out of the tangled web of vehicles. Before I could chant "Repent Ye, Oh Wanton Woman," the car was on the main road, and I was on my way to thumb my nose at the seventh commandment.

I pushed a button on the CD player. Music of the 50's filled the air.

"I was trying to psyche myself up for the party," Ted said in answer to the face I made.

"Yeah, okay, so that would explain things if we had gone to high school in the 50's, which we didn't. Are you trying to make me feel even more ancient than I do?"

"True we weren't in school in the 50's, and you, gorgeous one, are definitely not ancient. I chose these CD's because I like the music, and I figured that listening to any songs older than today's tunes, would get me into the proper mood for a reunion." His smile was triumphant.

"Hey, I remember this one," I said. "Peggy Sue. That was by Buddy Holly, wasn't it?" I turned the volume control higher and the car nearly rocked with the sound.

"Sure was." He smiled as I soaked in the lyrics. "And here's a song I think they might have written just for you."

He pressed one of the many controls and suddenly the car was filled with the strains of "It's my party and I'll cry if I want to..."

"You could cry if you want to, Bea. It might help. I'm here for you, you know."

"I don't need to cry," I replied indignantly as the tears rolled down my face.

Ted slowed the car and carefully pulled over onto the side of the road. He put his right arm around my shoulder and pulled me close, or at least as close as the gear shift would allow."

"Your gear shift may make my plan to seduce you harder than I thought," I said.

"Oh, Bea," he answered.

Oh, Bea? Was "Oh, Bea" all any man could ever think to say to me?

So what did it mean this time? Oh, Bea, a minor thing like a gearshift could never keep me away from your hot body. Or: Oh, Bea, I've dreamed about this moment for twenty-four years?

No, more likely it meant: Oh, Bea, you need to face it. Nobody wants a broken down old Ford. I've got my eye on a sportier model, like the one Dick found.

"I'm sorry," I sobbed. "I know I'm not much to look at. I know you don't desire me. I..."

"Hey, hold on a moment. I never said anything about not desiring you. I do desire you. I always have and I always will desire you. If I thought it would make you happy, I would keep on driving and never return to Moorestown."

He sighed and when I did not say anything he continued: "I told you before we left the house, but I don't think you understood that I would do *anything* to please you. The problem is, Bea, I think what might seem as if it would please you right now, would not please you later."

I leaned against him. I felt the warmth of his body and the rhythmic beat of his heart. His breath danced on my skin. He buried his face in my hair. I had not been this close to another man for decades. It felt so unbelievably sensual and I did not want it to end. I wanted to be desired. I wanted it badly. But sadly I knew Ted was right about how I would feel in the morning. I had to try and make things right at home. I had to go back and tell Dick that I heard him on the phone with Mercedes. Then to use one of Dick's favorite expressions, the ball would be in his court.

I pulled away. "One kiss," I said, "for old time's sake."

"One kiss for old time's sake," Ted murmured before he pulled me back and lowered his face to mine.

It might have been just a kiss, but as kisses go it was incredibly delicious, perhaps because it was from the start the acknowledged beginning and end of our liaison; but in reality I think for deeper reasons as well.

As our lips touched, the tension seemed to drain from my body. I felt Ted's arms move around me, and I relinquished myself to their strength and their tenderness. All of my senses were focused on that moment.

His was a gentle kiss at first, but harder and more demanding as the seconds passed. There was no hesitation, no ambiguity. I tasted the salt of his lips. His tongue moved slowly forward and touched my own, a sampling, a startling promise of things to come. A kiss – just a kiss – yet it spoke of lust and love and opportunity.

The haunting sound of *Unchained Melody* surrounded us. I did not hear the truck as it careened wildly toward us, did not see the horror on the driver's face, as he pumped frantically on the brake petal. An instant before tons of metal slammed into the side of our car, meshing our fractured bodies into the mangled roadster, our lips parted, and I smiled contentedly. Maybe I'm not a sports car, I thought, but life just might not be so bad for this old Ford.

CHAPTER 19

Have you ever startled to conscious awareness while driving, absolutely oblivious to your destination? You stare at the road in front of you. Then suddenly a synapse fires and the answer is clear: Ah yes, you say, as if you are not sitting alone in your car, I was on my way to the grocery store or to work or to fetch a child from ballet or little league. A moment is spent assessing the damage. Are you on the right road? Going in the right direction?

That is how I felt as I looked around the hallway where I was seated next to Ted, he on one gray metal chair, I on the other.

I saw nothing that identified the building itself, only enormous azure blue numerals on the wall proclaiming that we were on floor twenty-five. I did know that we were in a hospital because I remembered sounds of a crash and the image of twisted wreckage that was once a brand new car. I also could visualize ambulance drivers and EMT's in flowing white uniforms.

What was disconcerting however was that the areas I could see did not look like any medical facility I'd ever visited.

Everything was outrageous, over-the-top, excessive. It looked more like a Donald Trump hotel on steroids than a hospital. The walls were painted an eerie florescent mother-of-pearl gloss and the ceilings stretched so high above our heads that I could not see the fixtures. Or perhaps it was the brilliance of the light coming from those enigmatic fixtures that gave the sensation of looking up into eternity.

We must have been flown here by life flight helicopter, I thought. I recalled watching the burning wreckage from above, a mangled pile of metal and glass. I struggled to remember more details. For an instant I could almost feel the shock of impact, and then I could feel nothing at all.

God we were lucky, I thought. We should both be dead, and if not, we should look a damn sight worse than we do. I glanced fearfully down at myself, and then at Ted. No blood, no obviously broken bones, no bandages, no casts.

"Are you okay," I asked quietly.

"Yes, Bea, I am. Are you?"

"I seem to be, but how? Did you see your car, Ted? Your beautiful new car! Destroyed."

He shrugged. "I saw it."

"Oh, God, Ted, you just bought it days ago. Were you insured?"

"Don't worry about such things, Bea. I'm just so glad you are here. I didn't know if you would be."

"Yeah, I guess they could have taken us to different hospitals. Well, maybe they only had one helicopter and had to use it for both of us, or maybe this is the main trauma center for the southern New Jersey area. Although I can't say I'm too impressed with the care so far. I mean granted we look okay, but what if one of us is bleeding internally or we go into shock or..." I could feel my anxiety level rise.

"Bea."

"What?"

"Breathe."

I leapt out of my chair at that.

"Breathe? That's your advice? We have just survived a major car accident. At any moment some undetected internal injury could kick in and kill one of us. If not, if we live, I have to explain to Dick, and I might add to my parents – both of whom have practically disowned me already for failure to keep my husband's affections – why I was parked in a car with an old boyfriend, when I am supposed to be working my butt off to save my marriage. My friends will think I'm immoral, and my daughter will blame me even more than she already does for the breakup of our family. Dick will probably seize this opportunity to dump me and look like a hero. Mercedes undoubtedly is already moving her four-poster lagoon of iniquity and her skimpy little thong bikinis into my house! And you want me to relax and breathe?"

A shadow loomed above us. I sat back down. Ted did not.

"Ted. Welcome back," the voice boomed.

The two grasped at each other's arms in the way men sometimes do in lieu of hugging.

"Thanks. Good to see you again too, Bernard. Meet my friend Beatrice." Ted waved at me with exaggerated enthusiasm.

I stared at the large burley man who stood before me. His white garments were sweetly reassuring. Finally we were going to receive the medical attention we deserved.

"I have to call home," I said, getting up out of my chair.

"Clarence will help with your arrangements, Beatrice. But I would like to welcome you to level twenty-five. I know the first time here is always a bit overwhelming."

He smiled. I did not return the favor.

"I've never been to any trauma center," I replied with a growing impatience. "And I must say that I am unimpressed with the quality of care."

Ted gave Bernard a look I knew so well. I had seen that very 'aren't women cute when they are being difficult' look on his face when he was talking with my dad.

"Clarence is going to facilitate her?" Ted asked.

"Yes," Bernard answered with just about the widest grin I'd ever seen.

"That would be something to watch."

"That it would, Ted. That it would. Unfortunately you are due up on level twenty-eight, so best bid your friend goodbye."

Goodbye? Wait a minute. I don't think I like the thought of Bernard and Ted leaving without me.

"Hey, how about I go with you until someone decides what tests I need? I don't think I should be left alone here. What if I develop some unexpected medical emergency? Can't this Clarence fellow come and get me from, what was that floor, twenty-eight?"

Ted moved from Bernard's side to mine. "Bea, listen to me," he said. "You need to stay here on twenty-five. You will understand soon enough. Trust me, everything will be fine. Just listen to Clarence and follow your heart when it comes to big decisions. And after you choose, dearest Bea, I hope you will always try to enjoy something about life just as it is each day."

"I know, I know," I said, finally smiling just a small smile. "I shouldn't spend my life waiting for the blue light special."

"That's true, Bea. Try to remember that," he said without the laugh or smile I anticipated.

"Jeez, Ted, you sound so serious. We aren't parting forever, you know. I'll probably still be sitting here when you get back from X-ray or wherever Bernard is taking you."

Ted did not answer. He simply looked at me with longing and something akin to sorrow.

"We have to go, Ted." Bernard seemed annoyed.

Ted reached out one arm and placed a hand on my shoulder. "Bea, I don't know if we will ever see each other again."

"Not planning to attend the next class reunion, are you?" I shook my head in mock seriousness. "Afraid I'll kidnap you again and make you wreck another car?"

"Hush. Listen to me. I don't have but a couple seconds, so I want you to focus. I have faith that your life will be everything you could ever want it to be. I wish I could be in it with you, but that is not too likely. If I could be though, I would. I would love you and take care of you and fill your world with daffodils."

I stared at Ted. Daffodils or simply daffy? Suddenly I understood why Bernard was so anxious to transport Ted upstairs, and why I could not accompany them. Ted obviously had serious neurological damage from the crash. He was talking gibberish and I was frightened.

I looked down at my hands, then I raised my head to tell him to take care of himself and not to worry about me. But I was too late. Ted and Bernard were gone, vanished without a sound. I was alone, and to make matters worse, I was alone in a hospital designed by The Donald.

CHAPTER 20

"Beatrice Kelly?"
"McBane."
"Pardon me?"
"My name is Beatrice Kelly McBane. Kelly is my maiden name. My insurance is under my married name, which is McBane." This better not be Clarence, I thought, or it will take hours to fill out my paperwork.

"Well, welcome, Beatrice Kelly McBane." He smiled as he emphasized my married name. "I am Clarence, and I am here to welcome you to level twenty-five."

Ah, I thought, that explains it. Clarence is just a greeter. Don't have to be the sharpest knife in the drawer for that.

"So, Clarence," I said, trying not to show how anxious I was to finish with his role in my admission process. "What are the chances that you could direct me to a telephone?"

He ignored my question as he shuffled through a pile of papers.

"May I call you Beatrice?" He spoke with such seriousness that I struggled not to say something too harsh in reply.

"Fine. Sure. Whatever. But I really need to phone home. When the accident is reported on the news, Dick – that's my husband – and my parents will figure out that Ted and I were in the crash, and they need to know that I'm okay; or at least that I seem okay, since no on here seems interested in testing to find out one way or the other." I swallowed vigorously in an attempt to keep panic from overwhelming me.

He smiled and continued as if I had not spoken. "Beatrice, I need to explain where you are and why," he said.

"Well, let me make it really easy for you, Clarence. I'm in a hospital. I'm not so shook up from the crash that I haven't figured that out. Now I assume all insurance forms have to be filled out before you let me near any exits, so I can't run off without providing the hospital administration an opportunity to charge my insurance company five or six times more than they should for services performed, or not performed," I added spitefully. "All I want to do is make one simple phone call first. So show me where the telephones are!"

I knew I should not shout at the old guy but I was getting really angry.

"I cannot do that," he said calmly.

"Then get me a supervisor!"

"Oh dear; oh dear. This is always the hardest part." Clarence sighed deeply and I began to feel a bit sorry for my outburst. He was a just a sweet old man attempting to inject some relevance into what I was willing to bet was a pretty colorless life. I tried to sound less threatening.

"Look, Clarence, I'm sorry I yelled at you. It's just that I am worried about my family." I lowered my voice even further and spoke slowly. "I was in a bad accident, and I've been brought to a hospital that is obviously some distance from my home. I had no identification with me because I left a party unexpectedly, so the hospital probably hasn't notified anyone that I'm here. Nobody knows where to find me. I need to contact them. So you see why I need you to show me where I can call them?"

"I understand, but no can do."

"No can do? No can do-oo? Look mister, I've tried to be nice, but you are being just a bit too dictatorial for a hospital greeter! Take me to a fucking telephone, and do it now before I have you fired or whatever they do to incompetent old volunteers!"

"I cannot take you to a telephone, Bea. There are no phones here, and your family knows what happened to you. There was a significant time lapse between the accident and your arrival here. Your family members know. They have already grieved for many weeks."

"Grieved? What do you mean grieved?" The idiot was talking as if I was comatose or worse, dead! I certainly was neither. I could think. I could feel. I could yell and be nasty. I was definitely alive.

"Get me your supervisor immediately," I barked.

"Bea, there is no supervisor; at least not one who communicates directly with pilgrim souls. Not until a soul reaches level forty can there be even minimal direct contact with the Supreme One, and few have arrived there yet. Trust me."

Trust me? Why is it that the least trustworthy of the sexes is so fond of that phrase? Well I no longer trusted men in general, and I certainly did not trust Clarence, but I figured I'd met my match for stubbornness, so I decided to humor him, at least until someone else showed up.

"Okay, Clarence," I said, aiming for sweetly submissive. "What is the next step? Where do we go from here?"

"That's my girl. Let's sit down over here and I will answer all your questions."

He led me through a doorway into an office I had somehow missed seeing, even though it was directly in front of me. Ted is not the only one who should be having a brain scan I thought. Clarence gestured toward a large chair.

I lowered my body down into the softest most luxurious cushions and closed my eyes for a second. When I opened them, Clarence was seated at a grand desk, a desk of well-oiled walnut and gold trim – a desk I had not noticed just moments before. Brain injury? Optic nerve damage? Post-Traumatic Stress Disorder? I did not know what was wrong with me, but I was now certain that something was. I had better cooperate so I can get some medical attention, I thought.

Clarence cleared his throat and began. "You, dear Beatrice, are about to embark upon a most magnificent journey."

Oh I bet I am, I thought. CAT scans, thick tasteless liquids to drink, needles stuck in, blood sucked out. Yep, I definitely was about to begin a most magnificent journey.

"But before you can begin that journey," he continued, "you must comprehend where you are and why, and what comes next. Shall we begin?"

It was truly difficult to maintain a pleasant tone, but I was determined to finish with Clarence and get some help.

"Yes," I said. "Let's begin."

He wiggled the mouse and stared at his computer screen. "It says here you were raised Lutheran."

"Roman Catholic."

"Pardon me?"

"I was raised Roman Catholic."

"Darn computers. Please excuse my language, Beatrice."

"I'll survive."

"Of course you will." He smiled. I wanted to strangle the sweet old fellow.

"Beatrice, whether you were raised Lutheran, Jewish, Mormon, Presbyterian or Roman Catholic, it matters not to us, except that my explanations will need to be slightly different to allow for your knowledge base. That is why I asked."

I began to wonder if Clarence was a psych ward runaway. I smiled my most soothing smile, just in case.

"Do you remember the biblical verse: there are many rooms in my Father's mansion?"

"Of course. It means that there is room for all of us in heaven, for all the little children in the world..." I began to sing: "yellow, red and black and white, we are precious in His sight. Jesus loves the little children of the world." I smiled and waited for the applause of a return smile.

Clarence did not seem to find my performance amusing. In fact he did not even hint at a smile. "That is one way to interpret it, however it really means that there are many levels in every soul's journey and you, my dear, have arrived at level twenty-five."

No question. The old geezer was daft!

"So I am at level twenty-five. Can you tell me what that means?" I figured I was safe if I could keep him talking until the guy with the net arrived.

"Yes!" He seemed quite pleased with my question. "Each level represents a development of the soul, a growth toward a perfection that only One will ever attain, but to which all should aspire. You have developed through many lifetimes into a soul worthy of the privileges of a twenty-fifth level pilgrim. Do you have any questions on what I have explained so far?"

"Yes. Don't you think we should get the insurance information into the computer system so I can get some X-rays and other tests, and then you and I can take all the time we want to talk about the twenty-five levels of development."

"Not *the* twenty-five levels, Bea. There are many more levels than that; but you have just reached the twenty-fifth and that is a major milestone. Would you like to know what it means to be a soul on this level?"

I took a deep breath. Clarence would finish his sorry tale if I were bleeding to death in front of him, so I guessed I might as well cooperate. "Yes," I replied with what I hoped was sufficient enthusiasm. "I would love to know."

"It means you can choose to return to earth with a specific goal. You might want to search for a cure for cancer or some other disease. You might long to fight homelessness or to bring honor back into government, although that last one is not an easy task…"

He was standing directly in front of me, leaning against the desk's edge. I had not seen him move from his chair to the front of the desk. I must be blacking out for short periods of time, I thought.

"And most importantly, Beatrice, unlike your previous lives, you do not have to begin this one as an infant unless you choose to. Once you decide what you want to accomplish, you can request to begin your next life as an adult. You can get right at your quest without waiting to grow up. That does not mean you are guaranteed success, just an optimum opportunity to achieve your goals."

"I don't have to begin life as an infant?"

"No."

"I just pop on down as a fully functioning adult?"

"Exactly!" He sounded delighted!

"So wouldn't people be aware that I had no childhood?"

I could not believe I was conversing with daffy man as if he were sane, but I wanted to understand his obsession with this level theory. I smiled cheerfully and waited for his answer.

"Bea, when did you meet your husband?"

"When we were in college," I answered cautiously. It might not be a good idea for Clarence to gain too much knowledge about my family, I decided.

"You did not know him as a baby, then?"

"No, of course not."

"As a child even?"

"No-ooo."

I could never have worked in the mental health area. Five minutes in Clarence's company and I was ready to scream at loony guy to get to the fucking point.

He paused for a moment observing me. I must have passed his test for witlessness, because he continued. "But you believed he had been a baby and then a child, even though when you first met him, he was a fully-functioning adult?"

"Yes, I believed that. That is how we all get to be adults. First we are babies, then children, then adults." Clarence scrunched his features together in what I could only assume was a gesture of scorn for my need to state the obvious.

"Anyway," I said, perversely anxious to win the round, "I saw photographs. I met his parents. He did not just materialize onto the basketball court."

"And how do you know that his parents were his parents?"

"He introduced me. I met people who knew them."

"Ah ha! What if you met no one but Alfred; would you still have believed that he had been a child, that he had parents?"

"Who?"

"Alfred," he answered impatiently.

"Who the hell is Alfred?"

"Your husband."

"You mean Dick."

"Who is Dick?"

"Richard Fallsworth McBane, the third, or Dick for short and descriptive of his character."

He stared at me, eyes void of comprehension. His medications must be powerful, I thought. I tried again with fewer words: "Clarence, my husband's name is Dick."

"Dick!" He spit the word. "Is anything in the report correct? Stupid technicians."

Clarence returned to his computer. His eyes moved across and back, up and down, line to line. His face was expressionless at first; then ever so slowly, a look of rage, unlike any I'd ever observed, turned his angelic countenance into a horrific mask of anger.

"Stay there," he thundered.

No problem complying. The last place I wanted to be was wherever Clarence was headed. Nice old volunteer geezer had transformed into a cross between Moses and Lucifer, and I just knew some technician in hospital admitting was about to regret a keyboarding error big time.

CHAPTER 21

When I opened the infamous lingerie package, a lesson was ripe to be learned; a valuable lesson on respecting privacy and about what can happen when one looks where one should not. Unfortunately I am not a quick learner

Oh I sat there quietly for a while, and if Clarence had returned within a reasonable time frame, he would have found me waiting as obediently as a newly plighted postulant. But he did not return quickly, and after ten or fifteen minutes I vacated my chair. I wandered about the office. I noted that there were no windows, odd for an office with such exquisite furnishings. I spun his desk chair around. I played with the gold cherub pencil holder. I fingered the keyboard of his computer. That the screen flashed on to the file it did, was not my doing. That I read it was.

Pilgrim Soul: 25bfk-37p1045

Name: Beatrice Francis Kelly

Progression life #25

Most recent existence: White female, Lutheran, married, one child

Spouse: Alfred Laurence Kelly

Child: Laura Francis Kelly

Missions: literacy volunteer, AIDS activist, benefactor to numerous elderly and lonely persons

Notable qualities: charitable, forgiving, trustworthy, kind, loyal, cheerful

Notable physical characteristics: tall, coal black hair, green eyes

Recent ending: Crushed by car while assisting victims at crash scene.

The computer screen blurred. I returned to my chair and fell back into it. I could see her. A vision so clear that there was no denying its validity; a woman with green eyes and coal black hair; a woman named Beatrice. Her hand reached toward me through shattered glass, her eyes gentle and concerned, her voice soothing.

"Hold on, honey. The ambulance is on the way. Help will be here soon. Don't give up. Don't be afraid. I'm here with you." Her hand gently touched my forehead, brushing hair back out of my eyes.

"What is your name?" she asked.

"Beatrice," I whispered through waves of pain.

"Beatrice? Mine too. What's the chance of that; two women named Beatrice in the same place at the same time." She smiled and her kind eyes looked deep into mine willing me to survive.

"Don't be afraid," she said again. "I'm just going to go back up the road and watch for the ambulance because it is pretty dark out here. Can you hold on alone for a minute? I'll come right back, I promise. Don't worry. Okay?"

"Okay." I think I said the word. I know I thought it.

She touched my face once again with her gentle fingers and then she moved away. I've never felt lonelier than when that face disappeared from my sight. As long as she was with me I could lock onto her eyes and trust that she would keep the monsters away. I could believe that help would arrive in time to allow me to be a mother to my two sweet children.

But the instant her eyes were gone from sight an icy certainty encompassed my body. I felt no pain as darkness settled over me easing my way. Then suddenly, piercing that darkness, two bright lights flashed into my window. I heard the squeal of tires and a terrible thud, and then the flames began, and I thought, thank God for the warmth. I am so terribly cold.

I remember next looking down from the air. Flames and black smoke were shooting upwards. Perpendicular to those flames I could see a truck and another car. The truck was crossways in the road, its cab meshed into Ted's car. The other vehicle was on its roof, its side resting against the cab of the truck. People swarmed about the wreckage. Mangled bodies were sprawled on the ground: Ted's body, a man I guessed to be the driver of the truck, and barely visible beneath the overturned car, a woman with coal black hair and green eyes.

Even as my mind fought to disbelieve, I knew. I knew where I was, and I knew I would never go home again.

Ted's parting words finally made sense. His goodbye was poignant because somehow he had understood that it was forever. I tried to swallow my grief but it surged upward violently and passionately.

"If only I had known," I sobbed. "If only I could have told him goodbye before forever began."

"That can be arranged. The harder problem is what we do with you, Beatrice Kelly McBane. You are not supposed to be here."

"I wasn't supposed to die?" I looked up into Clarence's eyes. I gave no thought to his soundless reappearance. Hope surged through my body. I could return home!

"Oh no, dear, there is not any supposed to be or not supposed to be involved in the dying order. Death happens when it happens, and we are not involved in any way other than as a celestial limo service." He emitted a laugh at that, obviously amused by his own humor. "No," he continued, "that is not what I meant at all."

"Then what did you mean?"

"I meant you were not supposed to be on level twenty-five. You are only a nineteen, Bea. Not bad. Not bad at all, but nowhere close to a twenty-five. It was an input error. The wrong soul was picked up for transport. It has happened before, but we always discovered the mistake in time to do a normal infant return. This was a major snafu. You should not even know about level twenty-five."

"I'm not evolved?"

"Evolved? Yes, absolutely! To this level? No."

I looked up at him from my chair. I could feel the tears well up in my eyes again. "What will happen to me then?"

"I don't know. The Supreme One is deciding. We should know shortly."

"Clarence?"

"Yes?"

"What about Ted? Is he evolved, or was he a mistake as well?"

"Ted a mistake? No, no, not at all. He is a good solid twenty-eight, although Bernard sent me a message that the lad is acting strangely. Keeps asking about you, long after transition should have dulled any feelings he might have carried with him."

I smiled at that revelation. Then the phone rang, a phone that until that moment had not existed.

Clarence lifted the mother-of-pearl receiver to his ear.

"Hello? Yes, Supreme One, she is right here." He smiled and nodded to me. His smile faded before the nod was completed. "Yes, of course. But, I... No. But, I... Well, could I just ask one thing? Fine. Why bother to listen to me. I'm just a Three-thousand-year-old angel. What do I know?"

He turned to me. His face held no comfort.

"What's wrong?" I asked, fearing that the answer would be a one-way ticket to Purgatory for the commandments I had considered breaking.

"You have been declared a level twenty-five," he snapped. "Seems the Supreme One is in the warm and fuzzy female frame of mind, and has decided that you've earned a six-level bye. I hate it when this happens. The world does better with good old-fashioned biblical scare. I miss fire and brimstone! I crave plague and petulance!"

"I'm a level twenty-five?"

"By declaration, yes. Certainly not by evolution." He sniffed a proper English butler sniff.

"Then, Clarence?"

"Yes?"

"May I see Ted?"

"Just turn around."

CHAPTER 22

Pure unadulterated joy coursed through every fiber of my being at the sight of Ted's face. Guilt was a close contender for first place.

"It's okay, Bea. There is nothing to feel guilty about," Clarence said.

I looked back at him with apprehension. The last thing I needed was a 3000-year-old angel reading my thoughts.

"Relax, I'm not reading your mind, if that's what you think," he said. "I simply am reading your face and body language. You just realized that you are feeling no sadness for the family and friends you left behind. Don't shake your head at me. It's true. I've been working the twenty-fifth level for centuries, and I've seen it happen again and again. It terrifies people and makes them feel guilty." He stopped and laughed quietly. "I do so love it when that happens. Guilt is my favorite human emotion. Anyway, the thing is that suddenly you grasp the fact that you do not miss anyone on earth. Feels wrong, but it is exactly right, and an inevitable part of the transition. One cannot be where there is pure joy and experience grief for what is left behind."

"If that's so, then why did I grieve for Ted when I thought he had said goodbye forever?" I challenged.

"Because you had not yet left him behind."

Clarence sighed one of his famous sighs, a habit that was wearing on me. I could envision the sands of the desert shifting with his every breath.

"So here is the drill. You two stay here. I have to spend some time working out the details of Beatrice's transition back to earth. It won't be easy, you know. Things usually occur in the order they are meant to here."

"I am sorry to be such a bother."

My sarcasm was wasted. He answered in a tone too serious to pass for humor: "Well, we have no choice but to deal with it now, so talk to Ted. Try to formulate any questions you have and when I return, I'll do my best to answer them."

With that he was gone. One second he stood in front of me, the next gone. No lag time in heaven, or whatever this place was called.

I turned to Ted.

"I am so sorry," I said. "If I hadn't wanted revenge, if I had let Dick's phone call with Mercedes pass without reaction, you and I would still be alive. My children would have a mother, my parents would have a daughter, and Dick would still have a wife to cheat on."

Ted smiled for the first time since our arrival in The Supreme One's mansion. "Oh, Bea, I'm glad your sense of humor survived the crash!"

I whispered the question I had to ask: "Are we really dead?"

"Dead is not my favorite word. It leaves me feeling claustrophobic and rather crawly. I prefer transitioning. To that revised question the answer is yes, Bea, we are transitioning."

Transitioning, a passing from one stage to another. The concept certainly was less frightening than the basic dust-to-dust image I'd carried since childhood, but it still did not make much sense to me.

"I guess you have done this three times already since you are a level twenty-eight. Pretty impressive. Only how did you hide the fact that you were so evolved when we were in high school?"

"Excuse me. I was pretty damn evolved for an adolescent male." He sounded truly insulted.

"Yeah, I guess you were evolved compared to most of the guys I dated." I stood quietly. I knew I could not give in to the temptation to take a slow stroll down memory lane. "So tell me," I said. "What comes next?"

"It's rather simple actually. You decide what you would like to do with your next life and whether you want to begin that life as a baby or an adult. Clarence will input your choices and other relevant information and within three or four earth weeks you are back in action."

Ted's words were preposterous, but I reacted as if they were not. Next to my dandy denial vault, my favorite defense mechanism is my Miss America smile. It comes in handy whenever reality is less than desirable. Sort of like when a contestant smiles warmly and announces: I want to work on my abs and help achieve world peace. You know and she knows that the statement is garbage – well, at least the world peace part – but she smiles and the audience applauds vigorously as if the foolishness she uttered is worth cheering.

"What did you want to do this last time?" I asked.

"I wanted to make a difference in the lives of people who believed they were without hope. I did not choose a specific plan of action, which is an option if you transition as an adult."

(Oh don't forget that you wanted to work on your abs and help achieve world peace, I thought.) I struggled to maintain some degree of calm.

"You chose to begin your new life as a baby?"

"Yes, I chose to return to earth as a baby."

"Why? Why did you choose that way? As a baby, I mean?"

"I wanted to re-experience the wonder of childhood." He answered.

I began to pace back and forth in a space that I distinctly remembered as having held Clarence's desk. What Ted was telling me was preposterous, yet I had to acknowledge that it was equally preposterous that we were seemingly unscathed from the accident. I took several slow deep breaths.

"I'm sorry," I said. "I just don't get it! If I choose to go back as an adult, how will anyone know who I am? That is an impossible scenario!"

"Bea, let me ask you something."

"Okay."

"Before you came here, did you believe in God?"

"Yes, of course."

"In life after death?"

"Yes."

"Virgin birth, resurrection, loaves and fishes, miracles?"

"Yes, yes, maybe not, and sometimes."

"You accept some things then that are beyond proof simply because you have faith."

"Yes," I conceded, "based upon faith, I accept some non-provable things as true."

"Then, Bea, why not suspend rationality and simply go on faith here? Can't you just accept that you can be transitioned as an adult, and that you will have friends and family who both know and love you?"

"No!" I stomped my foot for emphasis.

Ted frowned and moved toward me until we were close enough to inhale the same air and feel each other's expelled breath.

"Bea, look at me. Whatever happened between us in the past, whatever happens to either of us in the future, know this: I loved you. You brought joy to my life. Now I would like to help bring joy to yours, but you are going to have to trust me, Bea."

He put his hands on the tops of my arms and held firm. "Look at me," he repeated. "Have I ever lied to you?"

I pulled away and turned my back to him. I had to admit that he had not, at least to my knowledge, ever lied to me. Yet what he told me strained my ability to accept his words on faith alone. Besides I had trusted without question once and look what happened. I had lived my life believing that the golden rule not only was a good way to live but that it offered some guarantee of reciprocation. Be a faithful wife, have a faithful husband. Tell the truth; be told the truth. But that is not what happened. No, I thought, that is not what happened at all!

I could feel the anger softly simmer inside, the tiniest ember at first, barely perceptible, a twinge, a spasm of gastric juices. I had forgotten what the emotion felt like. A door opened just as the ember burst into a full-blown flame of gut-retching fury.

A roaring voice demanded my attention. "This is not good! This is not good at all!"

I jumped away from the voice. "Clarence! You have to stop sneaking up on me. You nearly scared me to death." I began to giggle. "Although, I guess it's kind of late for that..."

Clarence did not laugh.

"You were feeling vengeful," he barked indignantly. "Vengefulness has no place here. Why was it here?"

"I was remembering what Dick did to me." I lifted my chin and stared at him without wavering.

"This is not good. This is not good at all."

"I believe you said that just moments ago."

I could tell Clarence was upset with me, and I'd seen what he could become if pushed far enough, but I had to pursue the idea that had just exploded in my brain.

"Clarence," I said, my voice sounding as adolescent as I felt, "Ted said I could choose to go back as an adult with a specific purpose..."

"Yes, you can." I'd never heard exasperation communicated so curtly.

"Then I would like to return to earth as a young woman. I want to be thin, gorgeous, and oh yes, voluptuous. My goal, if you must know, is to do unto Mercedes what she did unto me."

"Ted, go to twenty-eight!" Clarence bellowed. "Woman, you sit and don't you dare move a muscle until I return!"

I intended to say something witty. Something to show Clarence that I was not scared, but both he and Ted disappeared before I could speak. Indeed, I wondered if either one had ever been standing beside me, or if it was all just a bad hallucination involving one dead boyfriend and the evil twin brother of the sweet old angel from *"It's a Wonderful Life."*

CHAPTER 23

I don't know long I waited for Clarence to return. Time did not appear to be a quantifiable dimension in the place I found myself.

I thought about what I had been told: outrageous drivel, all of it. But how else could I explain where I was, and that my body, if not my emotional self, was intact? I wondered if I would be more accepting of everything if I were supposed to be there. It was obvious I was not evolved by anyone's definition. Grief and anger still consumed me, emotions Clarence declared I should be incapable of feeling. How was it he described the lack of sadness for those left behind? I searched my brain and found his words: One cannot be where there is pure joy and experience grief.

No grief. Yet I grieve, and I do so for the most shameful reason: not for people left behind, but for the loss of fidelity. No grief, Clarence said, but also no vengefulness. Vengefulness has no place here. Yet it exists within me. How terrible to be where there is pure joy and be a vessel for vengeance and hatred. Tears poured from my eyes.

"I do not understand," I wailed.

"It is not for you to understand."

Clarence stood before me. This time his voice was soothing. There was no fury, only what sounded like compassion.

"It has been a long time since I've walked the earth," he said. "While you waited I was sent to the place you think of as home to re-experience the power of human emotions. Every mile I traveled, through climates hot and cold, in cities and remote villages, the pleasure and pain that man experiences became my own. I sat beside a small boy in a schoolyard, a scrawny fatherless child who believed himself incapable of everything he deemed worthy. I cried out in rage as he relinquished the abundant merit of his being to the carelessness of others."

Clarence wiped a tear that escaped his right eye. He shook his head sadly and continued: "I breathed the fear in a man who knew he would lose his job and all hope of feeding his family, and in a woman facing a mortal's disease. I supped on the glorious passion of lovers young and old, and tears from my eyes blended with those of a woman mourning the death of the man she loved. All those things I had forgotten and know again."

He touched my shoulder without moving his arm. "I now understand once again the Supreme One's tenderness for you. You are to be allowed to return to your hometown. It will be a temporary placement, three weeks with no renewal."

He cocked his head to the side and observed me with wary attention. "Do you understand, Beatrice? What you have asked will be granted."

I nodded, unable to speak.

"What you do with what you are given is within your control. At the end of three earth weeks you will either return here in full status to be transitioned, or your soul will be placed in an infant yet to be born. It all depends on you."

"I'm going home?" The words barely escaped my throat before it closed with emotion.

"But not as the person you were when you came here. You understand that, do you not? Beatrice exists no longer except in memory of those who love her."

Did I understand? No. But I did believe.

"Who will I be then, if I am not myself? Will I have a name?"

"Your parents christened you Beatrice, which means bringer of joy. What would you think of being called Joy?"

"Joy," I whispered. The name felt warm on my tongue. I shook my head affirmatively.

"Alright then. You will return as Joy. On the day you arrive, it will be nearly three months past the death of Beatrice McBane."

"But it can't be that long. It just happened this very day," I protested.

Clarence shuffled his papers and continued as if I had not spoken. "It is late August. Your children are returning to school."

"Ben and Kelly." I spoke their names slowly, deliberately, as if awaking from a coma. "Who has cared for them?"

"Your parents, your husband, two women named Jane and Lorna. And a young woman named Joy."

"Won't they recognize me?"

"No. You will be a young woman with the body you requested." He paused for a moment and sighed heavily. I knew that part of my request still troubled him. "When you arrive," he continued, "you will know who you are and your role will be clear to you."

"And everyone will just accept that this Joy person has a right to be there?"

"Yes. I know it is difficult, but try to put aside your worries on this, Beatrice. No one will doubt your identity. Getting you there and recognized is easy. The difficult part belongs to you."

I waited silently.

"You see, Beatrice, if this were a permanent placement, you would be aware of your transition for a minute or at the longest, two minutes. During those brief moments a transitioned soul knows both past life and present. And then in a heartbeat, all past knowledge is gone, not even a fleeting memory remains, not even a feeling of having been somewhere before. From that moment until the new life ends, the person forgets about this place and about everything from past lives."

"But I will remember?"

"Yes, unfortunately you will. In a temporary placement, all knowledge of past and of this place remains. It is a formidable burden."

"You mean I will know who I really am, but everyone else will think I am someone else?" I bit my lip as I waited for his answer.

"Exactly. And listen very carefully now, because this is important." His voice became even more commanding. "You must never, I repeat never, communicate anything about this place or about your real identity to anyone. Even begin to do so and your placement will be ended instantly. Before the first syllable leaves your mouth, you will be recalled. There will be no mercy. There can be no mercy. That is the rule and it is unbendable."

I fought the apprehension that his words brought. "If there are rules, does that mean this is a common thing, this temporary placement?"

"Common? No. Absolutely not. Just the opposite. The reasons for temporary placements are complex and rarely does anyone below level thirty have need of one."

"But sometimes people do?"

"Yes."

"And have many had to be recalled?"

"A handful."

He smiled again. "Perhaps more than a handful, although fewer in recent years. But even with improvement, some will fail. It is not an easy task, to keep quiet about something so wondrous." He paused. "You said once that I reminded you of an angel in a movie."

"I don't remember saying that," I replied.

Clarence grinned. "Okay, maybe I do read minds, just occasionally."

I laughed.

"I said, or rather I thought, that you remind me of a hapless angel from a movie we watched every Christmas. I think it is mostly just that you have the same name, because the physical resemblance is not all that great, or at least not once we got beyond your bumbling persona back when I thought you were a hospital greeter."

"Ah yes, you did have some interesting ideas about me then."

"I thought you only read minds occasionally."

"Maybe a bit more often."

I was beginning to warm up to the old fellow. "Yes, I can see that. So what about the angel in the movie?"

"Long before that movie was created, a few sentences were spoken that should not have been. The offending soul was recalled, but the damage was done. Knowledge remained with the recipient, although only as a vague idea, a wisp of truth that disguised itself as imagination. Actually the Supreme One was amused by the results, especially by my fictional counterpart's bumbling behavior, as you put it, nonetheless the rules have become more rigid since then. There will never again be time for even a few words to be uttered. Do you truly understand that?"

"I understand. I truly do."

"Good. Now there is something else I have to tell you, Beatrice, something extremely troubling."

I waited for what I somehow knew was coming.

"Ted has requested a temporary placement as well. He pleaded for the opportunity to watch over you during your three weeks. He argued that he should have helped you to stay home the night you were killed, and he is right, he should have. But he did not have responsibility for your decisions. No one ever has responsibility for another adult's decision. He should understand that by now. He should not have asked for what he did, and in my humble opinion, what he asked for should not have been granted."

"But it was?"

"It was. It was." Clarence moved his head back and forth in obvious dismay. "I understand neither the request nor the answer. Ted risks so much. I cannot comprehend why he would choose to do so."

I thought about how carelessly I had hurt Ted those many years ago, and how he had offered his hand in friendship nonetheless. No vengeance in his heart.

Not so with me. My desires encompassed everything vengeful and nothing loving. The taste of revenge filled me. The search for that elusive substance had already claimed one terrible price. Ted's death was a direct result of my jealous rage, and yet he had just offered even more than he had already lost to try and protect me from my decidedly un-evolved self.

Of the many things I did not comprehend, Ted's friendship was one. I looked directly into the eyes of an angel and shrugged. "Nor do I understand his request, Clarence," I said. "Nor do I."

CHAPTER 24

I shivered in amazement at my image in the mirror. Damn, I look incredible. My hair is the color of honey fresh from the hive. Red was nice, audacious even, but this is better. I like the way the color frames my face. I like my face. I love my butt and my gloriously firm stomach. But most of all, Clarence, thank you, thank you! I adore the cleavage. Breasts rule!

Clarence said I would know instantly who I am, and I do. My name is Joy Anson. I'm 19 years old, and I have been working as a nanny for my, that is for Dick and Bea's children for over a month. Only how can that be, I thought, when I just got here at this moment? Was I here before I was here? What am I thinking; that's impossible. But then how can any of this be possible?

I finished washing Dick's New Jersey Devil's mug and rinsed it before placing it top down on the dish rack. I felt his presence before I heard his voice.

"Joy?" His voice was pleasant but casual. Love filled my lungs and coursed through my veins. That he could not feel its reflection amazed me.

"Yes, Mr. McBane?"

"I wondered if you might stay late and eat dinner with the kids today? I have football practice until six and Merci has been bugging me to take her to a new Chinese restaurant that just opened over on Lloyd Street."

"Gosh, sorry, Mr. McBane, I have plans. I could probably stay about forty-five minutes longer but that isn't long enough for you guys to go to dinner. How about I leave here at six-forty-five and drive the kids to meet you at the restaurant? That way the two of you can have a drink and a little time alone, and then Merci can bond with the kids over dinner."

He looked at me with undisguised skepticism. "Do you actually believe they will ever bond, as you put it, with her? They consider her the arch enemy."

I realized that Dick was right. Ban and Kelly hated Mercedes and even though they hardly knew this Barbie doll I had become, they adored me. This might be easier than I anticipated. I wanted Mercedes out of the house and out of their lives; and it seemed as if she was already well on her way, at least with Ben and Kelly. Piece of cake assignment: two kids down – one ex-husband to go.

"Oh I am sure it will just take time," I answered sweetly. "You go on to work and I'll tell them about the dinner plans before they go out to the bus."

"Thanks, Joy." The corners of his mouth stretched into his famous smile, the one that reeled me in a few decades ago and I could feel the blood rush south. I turned on the cold water and stuck both hands under the faucet to distract myself.

"Joy, please don't be so formal. My students all call me Coach. You could do the same if Dick is awkward for you. Mr. McBane makes me feel old."

"Dick is fine," I said with a smile. "And you don't seem old to me."

Can't let you feel old, I thought. After all I want you to dump a twenty-eight-year-old for a woman, who is just about to leave her teenage years behind.

"Good deal," he replied as he slipped into his sport coat.

"So it's a plan," I said. "I'll bring Kelly and Ben to the restaurant. You relax and enjoy your date until we get there."

He grinned broadly and waved as he walked away. The poor fool won't know what hit him.

I turned from the window at the sound of footsteps. "Well good morning, sleepy heads. Ready to go conquer the world of Moorestown's academics?"

"Oh, Joy, I don't feel well," Kelly whimpered. "Can't I stay home with you?"

"Sweetie, you know your dad said you have to go to school. I understand it's hard, I do, but it will get easier. Look I made pancakes the way you loved them when you were a little girl."

She glanced into the skillet and then stared at me with her luminous eyes, blue-green centers flecked with topaz, exact replicas of her father's, and asked, "How do you know what I liked? You weren't around here when I was little."

"Everyone likes Mickey Mouse pancakes," I said. "Who wouldn't know that?"

"Mercedes," she answered. "Last Friday night she stayed here. Dad said she came over early on Saturday, but I'm not stupid. She stayed all night in his room and I know what they were doing too." She flashed me a look of disgust.

"In the morning she made yucky French toast for breakfast – all slimy inside and burned on the bottom. But dad made me eat it. Be nice to Mer-cedes. Can't insult Mer-cedes."

Her words triggered a reaction so intense I had to fight to keep from running out of the kitchen. I struggled to clear my mind but the images burned relentlessly into my consciousness:

Mercedes touching my dishes, making French toast for my children. Mercedes in my bed, her libidinous sweat permeating my sheets. Mercedes in the bathroom, soaking in the tub after satisfying Dick's every carnal whim. Mercedes peeing in my toilet, marking it, claiming it all for herself: my house, my husband, my children! I swallowed the rage that boiled from stomach to throat.

I rinsed Dick's cereal bowl and loaded it into the dishwasher as I spoke, afraid my face would betray my distress if I looked at her. "It sounds like it was a difficult time for you," I answered in as calm a voice as I could muster. "Nevertheless, your dad is right to expect you to try and eat what she prepared. You were raised to be polite."

"You don't know how we were raised," Ben yelled. He had remained so quiet through the initial exchange that I'd forgotten he was there. "You don't know anything. You're just a stupid nanny!" He pushed his half-eaten breakfast away, grabbed his backpack off of the kitchen counter, and rushed out of the kitchen, slamming the door behind him.

The tumultuous racket was quickly replaced by dead silence. Kelly's voice broke that silence. "Ben doesn't really think you're stupid. He's just mad about Merci." She said.

"I know, Kelly. It's okay," I said. "This is tough for the two of you. I know you miss your mom." My voice failed me at that moment. I wanted to put my arms around Kelly and tell her that the part of her mom that really counted was at her side, but Clarence's warning was firmly planted in my mind: speak even the first syllable of a word about who you are and you will be recalled in an instant. It was a formidable threat. I pushed aside my desire to comfort and instead simply said: "I bet your mom misses you too."

Kelly put her fork down beside her plate and wiped her mouth. She sat quietly, eyes lowered, hands alternately clasped and unclasped in a rhythm that testified to her anguish. I watched as she worked through the conflict, her face solemn. It was a pattern so familiar. How could I not have mourned for her? How could hatred have been my only surviving emotion?

I watched her stand up. I watched her shift her weight – right foot, left foot, right foot, left. She frowned and looked up at me.

"Can I ask you a question, Joy?"

"Always."

"Do you believe in heaven?"

"Oh yes, Kelly, without a doubt!"

"And do you believe everyone goes there, even if they were doing something really bad when they died?"

"Do you mean people who kill or hurt other people?" I could not imagine what she feared. Did she think that her mom might be in a place with criminals?

"Are you worried about whether there are bad people in the place where your mom is?"

"No."

"What then?"

She shrugged. "I donno. Nothing. Never mind. I need to go." She gave me a hug, a quick careless grasp and release, and rushed out the door.

The action piqued my hunger. I wanted Ben and Kelly to be my children again. I longed to gather them within my arms, to smell them as I had when they were infants, to nuzzle my face against their heads and glory in the wonder of them. Instead I wrapped my arms around my chest and rocked gently back and forth, seeking the comfort I could not claim.

I remembered Dick's dinner plans just as Kelly reached the end of the driveway. "Kelly," I called out to her, "Chinese tonight at a new restaurant with your dad and…"

"Cool!" she yelled back before I could finish my sentence. She ran to the bus stop and turned once to wave before the bus pulled to a stop and whisked her from my sight.

CHAPTER 25

The doorbell rang while I was folding Ben's soccer uniform. I deposited it on the dryer and walked to the door. The body attached to the face that greeted me was encased in a brown and beige uniform embroidered with hideous pea green script proclaiming the company name: BUGS BE GONE.

"Morning, Miss," a cheerful voice proclaimed. "I am here to annihilate your ants."

"They are hiding in the pantry," I replied with a grin. The young man looked as if he might have had a bit part in the movie *Arachnophobia*, but his good humor was contagious. I waved him in and led him to the rear of the house. "I hope you aren't going to use anything too toxic," I said. "My kids, I mean the kids I sit for, are twelve and fourteen, and they spend more time on the floor than they did when they were infants."

"You can't have watched them that long," he said. "You hardly seem old enough to be watching them now."

"I'm old enough," I replied. "So exactly how toxic is the stuff you use?"

"Not to worry Miss. What I use is about as non-toxic as you can get – food laced with something that renders the little critters sterile. Not nice if they ever get the urge to procreate, but from everything I've read, ants don't spend much time worrying about the ticking of their biological clocks."

He seemed too attractive for a life as a hit man for bugs. My pulse quickened.

I seem to be rather easily aroused, I thought. I guess three months without sex can be frustrating, even for a celestial being.

"Do you ever mind your job?" I asked, trying to ignore the desire to throw myself at his wonderfully inviting body. "I mean does it bother you at all to be killing things day after day, even if it is just bugs?"

"Haven't been at it all that long," he answered.

I was somewhat un-nerved by that statement. Of course it wasn't as if his work involved brain surgery, or cosmetic dentistry, or even painting the house. How much harm could a fledgling exterminator do? Still I was in charge of the McBane household during the daytime hours so I was determined to be responsible. Despite the soft brown hair, the happy gray-blue eyes, the slender waist and the incredibly sexy smell of a man fresh from the shower, I could not ignore his abilities or lack thereof as an exterminator. I had to determine if he was competent before I allowed him to unleash his chemicals.

"Did you have to train for long before you could go out on your own to kill the little critters, as you call them?"

He looked at me with a serious expression and did not answer my sarcasm with his own. "Actually I sort of fell into the job," he said. "I came to Moorestown to help out a friend, and I needed something to do while I was here. The training was quick but sufficient, so please stop worrying. I assure you I am perfectly competent to spray your pantry and I promise I won't unleash any unnecessarily harmful chemicals or anything."

"Well, I'll leave you to your work then." I said. I did not think I needed to monitor his presence. He seemed unlikely to abscond with the cans of soup or boxes of fruit loops.

"Call if you need anything," I said as I walked away.

"Thanks, Joy," he answered. "I should be done in about ten minutes."

I was in the kitchen mindlessly grinding coffee when I realized what he had used my name, a name I have not told him when he arrived.

My knees buckled, and I reached for the back of a nearby chair for support. Clarence's exasperated declaration galloped through my head as I stood silently gasping for air. I could hear his words: "Ted has requested a temporary placement as well. He pleaded for the opportunity to watch over you during your three weeks."

"You know who I am." His voice was gentle and calm.

I turned and stared at the young stranger who was Ted. Tears ran down my face, tears of relief and mourning and love and fear. He did not come closer. He did not speak. Finally I shook my head yes and slumped down into the chair.

"So how is the master plan to nullify Mercedes coming?" His voice was light. He seemed to understand my tenuous hold on what seemed to be as close to sanity as I could find at the moment.

"Ben and Kelly don't much like her," I whispered. "Dick still seems to be enjoying her though."

"You still hate her? I was hoping once you got here that you might decide she is not worth risking your next life over – that instead you might give some thought to the benefits of progressing to another level."

I searched his face for condemnation. I found none, just the slightest hint of sadness and perhaps mild disappointment.

"Yeah, well you kill bugs for a living! What kind of progression is that?"

"I'm not progressing, Joy." He sighed. "You know this is just a temporary placement, so I can play guardian angel. And look, I know I should have asked you if it was okay, but there wasn't time. Are you angry with me? I promise I won't do anything to directly interfere with your revenge."

"Am I angry? Good question." I leaned forward and read the nametag on his shirt pocket. "Tom Gardengle. Cute. And now I've got both a Tom and a Dick in my life; I just have to find Harry and I'll be all set."

"Oh crap, you are angry, aren't you?" He sounded quite forlorn.

I relented a bit. "Not angry exactly; more overwhelmed with the whole situation. I don't want to be Joy the nanny. I want to be myself again. I want Ben and Kelly to call me mom. I want to be able to talk to Lorna and Jane without having them treat me like a teenage baby-sitter. I want to talk to Dick about what went wrong in our marriage. I want to understand what happened. And, damn it, Ted – I mean, Tom, I want that little tramp out of my house. I've barely had time to decompose and Dick is playing newlywed."

"I'm sorry," he said. "Sorry you were so hurt that the pain lives on."

"It hurts and it makes me angry. I wish I could do something!"

We stood there, both lost in thought.

"Remember the movie *Beetlejuice*?" I asked. "Winona Rider was in it and that actor who shouldn't have given up playing the part of Batman because he never did much of anything else."

"Yes, I remember it. Why?"

I sighed in frustration. "Darn I can't remember the actor's name! He played in another movie where he was cloned.

Keeton...something Keeton. Brian? Bruce? Well, anyway I feel like those ghosts, the ones in *Beetlejuice*. I'm here but no one really sees me."

Suddenly I giggled: "If only I had asked Clarence for the ability to do special effects. I could hide in Dick's bedroom. Just as he and little Miss cute ass are doing the deed, I could morph into a monster and scare the hell out of them. That could put a damper on their sex life."

Ted smiled, but he did not seem inclined to waste time on small talk. "What can I do to help, Joy?" he asked.

I walked to the counter and dumped the old coffee into the sink. As I rinsed the carafe I considered his question. What can he do to help? I did not have an answer.

My big plan is to make Dick turn away from Mercedes and toward me. But how? Despite my request for a perfect body, I find the thought of using that body to entice Dick somehow disturbing. I mean it isn't me. It would feel like cheating even if it was with my own husband! I sighed. This was an ideal topic for discussion with Jane and Lorna.

"Coffee?" I asked, waving the carafe at Ted.

"Absolutely!"

I finished grinding the beans and filled the reservoir with bottled water. As the aroma of freshly brewed coffee filled the kitchen I began to relax. I am alive. For a time, albeit an incredibly short time, I can see and touch and talk with Ben and Kelly. And I get to be with Ted for a little while longer before our next trip to Eternityville.

I filled two brown earthenware mugs with steaming liquid, added milk and started toward the table. As I walked across the kitchen, Ted's eyes examined my body, moving from painted toenails up over slender legs to hips that were gently curved. His eyes lingered at my waist and then moved toward my breasts,

breasts worthy of attention, perfect breasts on a perfect Barbie body. I waited for his reaction as his eyes slid slowly from left to right and back again. He finished his visual journey when his eyes reached mine.

"Not bad?" I asked.

"Not bad at all," he answered.

"A feast for your eyes?"

"You have always been a feast for my eyes," he said with no perceptible hesitation. He sipped his coffee and leaned back in his chair, eyes closed, his expression almost euphoric. "You know," he said, "if you declared the war over, we could have three glorious weeks together."

I considered his words. Three weeks to know I was wanted; three weeks without doubt or anger or jealousy. It was a tempting offer, an offer I knew I should accept. Yet the emotions that had propelled me back to earth on my mission of revenge remained as strong as ever. I stared at my hands, searching for the words to answer Ted. There was no need.

"It's okay," he said. "I understand. You have something you need to finish. Go do what you must. I'll be here if you need me, busy ending the lifecycles of millions of crawly creatures."

He held out a hand and I accepted it, his touch warm and gentle. The tears began to fall, traveling over my cheeks, along my nose, quiet screams of desperation.

"I am sorry," I whispered.

"No need for apologies," he answered. "I came to watch over you, and that is what I will do."

I closed my eyes and luxuriated in the peace of the moment. That moment did not last long. The doorbell buzzed with aggressive insistence. I wiped my tear-stained face with a terry kitchen towel and dragged myself to the front door.

"I can't find my keys. Have you seen them?" she tossed the words at me with no pretense of civility.

The smell of Boucheron was unmistakable. Did he buy it for her, or has she helped herself to my cosmetics as well as to my husband? I sucked air and moved back from her voluptuous form as if I'd been struck. Despite my new physique, I felt as vulnerable as I was that day in the foyer of her apartment.

I am royally screwed, I thought. I have no plan, scant time and the enemy is on my doorstep.

Mercedes flung off her coat and stared at my face.

"You've been crying," she said. "You look like shit. Boy trouble?"

Before I could answer Ted walked out from the kitchen. Mercedes smiled and saluted him with her ever-perky chest. "Wrong choice of words," she said with amusement. "This is no boy."

"Hi. I'm Merci," she purred as she sashayed past me to hold out a hand to Ted.

"Tom Gardengle," he answered politely. "I'm here to kill some ants. Guess I better get back to work. Thanks for the coffee, Miss." He smiled and walked away.

Merci watched him go. As soon as he disappeared from sight, she turned to me and grinned. "Nice ass. If he had a better occupation he'd be a great catch. Can't make much money killing bugs though."

"Money can't buy happiness," I replied, struggling for a casual tone.

She laughed and patted me on the shoulder. "No it can't, but it sure helps keep gloominess at bay. Anyway you go on with your work. I'm going to wander on up to the bedroom and see if I left my keys up there."

As I watched her walk down the hall and up the stairs, I knew my shot at immortality had just evaporated. God could not be pleased with the direction of my thoughts. The three-week-war for Dick's affection had begun and I would not rest until the enemy had been captured, drawn and quartered.

CHAPTER 26

I called Jane as soon as bug man and the sexpot completed their respective tasks and departed, and although Jane clearly viewed me as a member of a different generation, she responded expeditiously to my plea for help.

"So Mercedes upset you, Joy?" she asked as she started the porch swing moving with a firm push of her foot.

I handed her a glass of lemonade and chose a chair to her right. I longed to give her a giant hug, but I figured that might send her running home and me to an unemployment bureau in the great beyond. So instead of a hug, I paused as I handed her the glass and allowed myself one glorious moment breathing in the scent of Amour, the perfume I had given Jane for her birthday a short four months before the accident. In a situation with too few comforts, I found great pleasure in the fact that she was wearing it.

"That's a pleasant scent you're wearing," I said. "Mercedes wears a nice perfume also, although perhaps a bit too much of it. Anyway, I think she said it is called Boucheron."

Jane stiffened. "Boucheron was Bea's fragrance," she said.

"Wow. That's quite a coincidence."

Jane snorted her displeasure. "I would guess it is more like a lack of common decency on Dick's part," she answered. "Neither he nor Mercedes seem bothered by the need to act appropriately."

She looked away obviously embarrassed that she spoke so critically of Dick and Mercedes to an employee. I needed to think quickly or I feared she would leave.

"I know I shouldn't say so, her being involved with my employer and all," I replied, "but she struts around here as if they are married."

That did the trick. Jane's cheeks reddened.

"Stupid man," she said.

"Aren't they all?"

I noted the amusement in Jane's eyes and resolved to sound more like a nineteen-year-old. "Anyway, Mercedes just comes in as if she owns the place and she never fails to say something mean to me when she's here. I get really upset sometimes."

Jane smiled. "She often upsets me too, Joy, but did she do something especially upsetting this morning? Your call was rather confusing. You were talking a mile a minute. Let's see: you said Mercedes was flirting with an exterminator, that she was rummaging about in Bea's bedroom and that she upset Ben and Kelly. She did all that this morning?"

"Well, yes and no. She did drool over the exterminator's butt, and she was up in the bedroom looking for her keys, but I guess she didn't do anything this morning that affected Ben and Kelly. It's more that her general behavior is a problem, and I hate to see them upset by her. I've come to love them. They are such sweet kids and so vulnerable right now!"

"You're right, Joy, they are sweet and vulnerable," she said. She glanced impatiently at her watch. "But nonetheless, why this urgent call now? Why did you need me to rush over all of a sudden this morning if it is just her general behavior that concerns you?"

"I am sorry for asking you to drop everything and come over. I know you are busy. It's just that there is something I really need your advice on how to handle." I set my glass on the table and faced her. "This morning at breakfast Kelly told me that she was upset. She said Mercedes stayed in her dad's bedroom last weekend, and that she knew what they were doing."

"The little bitch is sleeping here all ready? Damn him!" Jane slammed her hand into the pile of pillows stacked in the corner of the swing. "Can't that man stop letting his penis act as his guide through life?"

I smiled. It felt incredibly good to be with Jane, just like the old days when I could share anything with her. I took a deep breath and reminded myself to be careful.

"But, Joy, I really don't see how I can help," she said.

"Well, the problem is that I don't know if I should say anything to Mr. McBane about how Kelly feels. I mean I don't want to do anything to harm his relationship with Mercedes, but his daughter seemed so upset..." I let my voice trail off.

"Nothing could disrupt that relationship short of financial ruin on Dick's part. Bea did her best, but while she was living one reality, Dick was living another: a world where you get to have both wife and girlfriend." The tears began to roll down her cheeks. She appeared oblivious to their journey, reacting only when her nose began to drip as well.

"I'll get you a tissue," I said. I hurried into the kitchen, glad for the opportunity to suck in a deep breath and shake my arms in a futile attempt to relax. I could not allow Jane to see that my emotions mirrored her own in intensity.

"Here," I said. "I brought you the whole box,".

"Thanks, Joy. The whole box just might come in handy." She wiped her face and blew her nose vigorously.

"God I miss Bea! She was my best friend and I am so angry with Dick. She did not deserve what happened."

"Why do you think it happened?" I asked. "I know it isn't really any of my business, but the kids talk to me, Kelly more than Ben, and it might help if I understood what happened." I knew it was shoddy reasoning. I just hoped Jane needed to talk as much as I needed to listen to her voice. She did.

"What happened is that Dick fell in love with a woman who had been a student teacher in his classroom about four or five years ago. Or maybe it was just lust. I frankly do not know. Whichever it was, after a couple weeks of clandestine dating, he settled the little tramp into a rent-free condo less than fifteen minutes from his own home. From that moment he stopped being the man we've all known; and I don't even like to talk to him anymore."

"Can't we do something to make him realize that his children need his attention? Can't we expose the roadster for what she is?"

"Bea would like you," Jane whispered. A smile slowly replaced the downward pull of her mouth.

"Why?" I asked, surprised by her comment.

"Well I would think for lots of reasons, but right this moment because you called Mercedes the roadster instead of Mercedes or Merci as Dick likes to call her. Bea rarely used Mercedes' actual name. She preferred names like Slutty or Lolita, and my personal favorite, Boobette."

I looked down at my chest. The sight still amazed me. "They are powerful things," I said as much to myself as to Jane.

"Like heat-seeking smart bombs," she answered, "instantly able to render most males incapable of rational behavior."

At that she rose and walked down the steps to her car. I followed her, trying not to let my disappointment show. At the bottom step she stopped and turned to face me.

"I am glad you are taking care of Ben and Kelly, Joy. Bea would approve."

"Thanks, Jane. You have no idea how much it means to me to hear you say that."

She opened her car door, climbed inside, and started the engine. Suddenly she rolled down her window and motioned to me. "You need to have a plan, Joy. Your time will fly by more quickly than you realize."

I took a step back from the car. A plan! Had she figured it out? Did she know who I was and what I intended to do?

"I need a plan?" I asked, terrified of her answer.

"Absolutely. I am glad you are here for Ben and Kelly, Joy, but you can't work as a nanny indefinitely. You should look into college courses; begin to make some plans for your future. Let's have lunch in a couple weeks. I'll talk with Lorna and call you. She was a career counselor before the twins arrived."

"I've always wanted to be a mom." I said. My words surprised me. I had not intended to speak.

"Just like Bea," Jane said, shaking her head, lips clenched. "You sound just like dear sweet Bea." She swiped one hand across her tear-covered face and steered her car onto the road with no further ado.

"More like Bea than you know," I whispered when she was gone. "More than you will ever know."

CHAPTER 27

"I hate you and I am not getting out of the car."

A band of angels could have gathered on the ledge formed by Kelly's protruding lower lip. She pulled her knees up to her chest and turned her face away from mine.

"I know you're upset that Merci is going to be at dinner, Kelly, but you can't stay in the car. I promised your dad I would have you here by seven and we are fifteen minutes late already."

My words met icy silence.

"Kelly, I am serious. You have to get out of the car!"

I heard footsteps behind me.

"Move, Joy." Ben scowled at me and flicked his head to command that I make room for him. "Come on out, Kelly," he said in a voice too old to have originated in a fourteen-year-old throat. "Dad will be pissed if you refuse to go in. Come on. You don't have to pay any attention to Merci." He held his hand out to her. I wanted to hug him. Instead I stepped further back from the car.

"Merci ruins everything!" Kelly's whining voice was a welcome sound.

"She can't ruin sesame chicken, Kelly." Ben spoke in a quiet tone, the way one might to a frightened animal or resistant toddler. "Let's go in. We'll order sesame chicken and fried rice. We can flick the rice at Merci when dad's not looking."

Kelly kept her legs firmly clamped against her chest, but she turned her head and I could see the slight promise of a smile, an elusive sunbeam across her stormy face. "We could kick her under the table and then deny it when she complains to dad," she said.

"Okay, maybe not that," I said, although I could think of a few carefully placed kicks I'd love to deliver myself. I drifted for a moment, mentally crouching beneath a restaurant table where Dick and Merci were seated, reveling in a daydream about placing spiders or fire ants on Merci's shapely ankles and watching them progress upwards. My dream back-fired when Dick stretched out his leg until his toes found her. I felt the all too familiar stabbing pain of a shattered heart as I watched his foot slowly move from ankle to shin to knee to slender thigh to...

"Joy! Hell-lo-o! Are you alive?" Ben was face to face with me, hands on hip, eyes open wide in exaggerated concern. "Kelly's already gone into the restaurant. Are you coming or should I go in without you?"

I searched his face for any sign that I'd spoken my thoughts aloud. The only emotion I could read appeared to be resignation. "I'll come in," I said.

The restaurant was classic New Jersey Chinese, the walls brothel red, the tables covered with white tablecloths and Zodiac place mats. Two fifty-gallon tropical fish tanks completed the vision.

Ben pointed to a table in the center of the room. I was relieved to see two sets of legs underneath, with four feet visibly attached to the floor. Kelly stood draped over her dad's left shoulder talking as fast as a twelve-year-old girl can. "Kelly seems happy," I said to Ben. "The crisis appears to be over."

"Yeah, for now, but wait until Merci starts to do her I-wanna-be-your-step-mother act. You haven't seen anything until you see Kelly react to that. You should stay and watch."

"I can't, Ben."

"Why not?" he asked as we reached the table.

"Hey dad." He pretended to punch Dick in the shoulder. Dick groaned as if he had been slugged.

"Joy can eat dinner with us, can't she?"

"Of course she can, but I believe she has somewhere she has to go. That is why she couldn't stay late and make dinner for you two at the house tonight," he answered. I watched for the light to come on when he realized that he just informed both kids that they were not on the A-list for dinner invitations. Nothing happened. Fortunately for Dick, his luck was better than his perceptiveness. Ben appeared too pre-occupied to react to anything, and Kelly was in her 'worship daddy' mode. As long as Dick remained before her eyes, he could do no wrong.

"Stay, Joy," she pleaded. "Please, please, please, please, please!"

"Don't be a pest, Kelly," Dick commanded in a no-nonsense tone. "Sit down next to Merci. She brought you a present."

That decided it. If the interloper was bearing gifts I needed to be there to protect my turf.

"I'd love to stay," I said.

Ben pulled a chair over from a neighboring table, slid it in-between Dick and Merci and gestured for me to sit with such sarcastic grandeur that I began to wonder if Ted had commandeered Ben's body for the evening.

"Waiter, we need another place setting," Dick said. His voice sounded pleasant enough but I recognized the controlled anger behind his civil tone. I ignored him and smiled widely at his playmate instead.

"So you have a present for Kelly," I said. "How sweet." (And by sweet, I meant as in the taste of a substance pretending to be sugar, such as aspartame or saccharin - fake sweet with an aftertaste and when taken in large doses capable of triggering diarrhea.)

"I do have a present," she replied. "Here, honey," she said to Kelly, removing a brightly wrapped package from her purse and holding it up for all to see. "Your daddy told me how difficult it is for you to start back to school every fall, and that ever since kindergarten your mom has given you what she called a 'brave girl' gift at the end of the first week of school. I know this isn't as nice as getting something from your mom, but I hope you like it anyway."

She moved her hand so that the box was within Kelly's reach. I wondered if Kelly would take it or slap it away. Her lower lip disappeared into her mouth and her eyes shimmered with moisture.

"Take your gift, Kelly," I whispered as I swallowed my jealousy that Mercedes could give my child what I could not. "Your mom would be glad that you got your 'brave girl' gift. She would want you to open it."

"Do you really think so?"

"Oh yes. I certainly do," I answered, nodding gently.

Kelly slipped the ribbon from the box and removed the paper. Her movements were deliberate and far too solemn for one so young. All that changed when she opened the box.

"Pierced earrings!" she cried out, her face a canvas of delight.

"Oh, daddy, does this mean I can get my ears pierced now? Mom said not until I'm thirteen. I would have been absolutely the only girl in school to have to wait that long. So does this mean I can get them done now, daddy? Does it? Oh please, please, say it does!"

Dick laughed. "Yes, kitten, you may get them pierced now. You can thank Merci for that. She convinced me that twelve is old enough. She'll take you to get them done at the mall on Saturday."

"Not the mall," I said too angry for caution. "That's risky. If it has to be done, I'll take her to the pediatrician's office."

"That is very generous of you, Joy," Dick said, sounding not even politely friendly, "but Merci and I have already decided how it will be handled."

He turned to Kelly. "Now if you will say a proper thank-you for the earrings, I'd like to call the waiter over and order. I'm starving."

"Me too, daddy! I want sesame chicken."

"And fried rice?" Ben asked pointedly.

"No, I don't think I'll have any fried rice this time," Kelly answered. She turned to Mercedes.

"Thank you so very much for the earrings and for talking daddy into letting me get my ears done. It is my best gift ever!"

Her best gift ever. My stomach lurched. I practically leapt out of my chair.

"Oh my God," I said. "I just remembered that I do have an appointment after all. Will you please all excuse me?"

"Certainly," Dick said. "I thought you said you were busy this evening."

"It just a dentist appointment." I forced a laugh. It sounded hollow. "I probably didn't want to remember it."

"Dentists are no fun. If it will help, you can come in a little late tomorrow morning," the future Mrs. McBane, gift-giver-extraordinaire, soon-to-be-step-mother-of-the-year, announced.

"I'll be over before Dick leaves for work with some fabric samples for those horrible chairs in the living room, and I'll be at the house until about 9:30 so I can make breakfast and get the kids off to school. If you aren't there when I leave, I'll stick a list of things to do on the refrigerator."

She gave a dismissive wave of her hand, shoved my empty chair away and moved her own closer to Dick's. The waiter approached in answer to Dick's summons and listened attentively as all four ordered with eager voices. No one appeared to miss me. No one even seemed to notice that I was still standing there. The circle had closed and was complete. I shut my eyes to their happiness and turned around. When I opened them I looked into the face of my guardian angel.

"This restaurant seems a little crowded," he said. "Besides, I've got a craving for pizza tonight. Join me?"

"Sounds heavenly," I replied.

CHAPTER 28

"This is sooooo good." I used my index finger to shove a small piece of pizza cheese back into my mouth. "Mom always told me not to talk with my mouth full," I said, smiling contentedly before I returned to chewing the pizza. "Course, there are probably different rules for the 'nearly departed.'"

Tom, a.k.a. Ted, emitted the longest sigh I'd ever heard. It put Clarence to shame and Clarence is a top-notch sigh-master.

"What?" I asked, although it probably sounded more like "wut" since my mouth remained over-loaded with sweet dough, warm gooey cheese and all sorts of interesting toppings. "You upset about sumtin?"

Tom stared silently at his untouched piece of pizza. His lack of gluttony annoyed me almost as much as his silence. I swallowed the now mushy glob of pizza, grabbed his glass of wine and downed it with a single gulp.

"Hey! You're under age!"

"Well my over-aged inner child wants wine."

I flashed a closed mouth grin, certain that all sorts of disgusting gunk covered my teeth. Ted did not grin back. I waved to the waiter and pointed to Tom's empty wineglass.

"Why the silent treatment?" I asked after vigorously using my tongue as a toothbrush. "Are you angry with me?"

"Angry? God no! I just feel so damn helpless. I came to protect you, and all I seem to do is watch every miserable moment you experience!"

"You watch my every miserable moment?" It was a ghastly thought. I definitely could not deal with the concept of him hovering over me while I sat on the toilet or shaved my underarms.

"Please tell me you didn't mean that literally!"

He laughed, and although I knew there was nothing of Ted's physical being in the body that sat across from me, I allowed myself to recognize the laughter as Ted's own.

"If you mean can I see through walls, catch speeding bullets in my hand and all that? I wish I could, sweet girl." He smiled and finally took a bite of his pizza. I watched him chew as if he were especially good at it.

The waiter arrived at the table, handed Tom a new glass of wine and asked me if I needed my soft drink refreshed. I could tell from the old guy's expression that he'd observed my consumption of the wine.

"I'm good," I said, trying for innocent but sexy. I smiled tentatively and looked up at him through half closed eyelids. Then I opened my eyes wider than was natural as I gently bit my lower lip between my teeth and ever so slowly released it.

The waiter was unmoved by my performance. He nodded formally and said in a remarkably stern voice: "Let me know when you need a refill on your Pepsi, Miss."

Tom smiled – actually smirked might be a more accurate description – and took a long leisurely drink of wine. He licked his upper lip, lowered the glass to the table and kept his hand on the stem.

"Afraid I'll steal it?"

"The thought occurred to me; and frankly, I'd rather not be arrested for providing alcohol to a minor. Such a waste of a good three weeks."

"Wimp!" I tried to look serious, but it was impossible. I smiled. He smiled back.

"In answer to the question you asked a moment ago, I cannot see through walls, or clothes, or take you flying above the earth," he said. "I am not a super hero. Hell, not only am I not a super hero, I am not even a very capable guardian angel!"

"That is a lot of nots. A person could get all tied up in them." I laughed. It felt good.

I reached my hand across the table and gently touched his. "Seriously, what could you possibly do to help? Dick is obviously quite in love with Mercedes, and Ben and Kelly are ready to forget they ever had a mother, or at least Kelly is. Mercedes bought her affection with a pair of 18K gold earrings."

"You can't really believe that. Don't you think you might be over-reacting?"

"Over-reacting? Let's see. I *believe* Dick is still in love with Mercedes. That could be over-reaction. However, I *know* she is wearing my perfume. Fact, not over-reaction. I *know* she is sleeping with my husband, in my bed, in my bedroom, in the house where my children live. Facts, pure facts. I only *believe* Ben and Kelly will soon forget me and love her; but I *know* she is wooing them with gifts, and I was there when Kelly declared the earrings to be the best gift she's ever received. Fact! Kelly said the earrings were her best gift ever, and she said it right in front of me, as if I don't matter, as if I don't hurt! How could she do that to me?" I shoved my plate away.

"Joy, look at me." His voice was insistent. "You are not Bea! To Ben and Kelly you are the baby-sitter, not their mom. Do you think they would have been sitting there ignoring you if they knew? You could never have left that restaurant if they knew!"

His words penetrated my brain, but rational thought lost out to the part of the brain that soaks-up and retains all of the heartaches we suffer in life. Anger grew – righteous anger, vindictive all-consuming anger.

Tom sat patiently for a short time then he turned around, waved to the nasty little man in the white apron and made a gesture as if he were writing a check. Grumpy nodded and rushed off to comply. He appeared to like Tom as passionately as he disliked me.

Nobody likes me, I thought forlornly. I waited until the waiter arrived at the table with his little brown leather check holder to reach for Tom's wineglass. I drank it and wiped my mouth with the back of my hand for good measure.

"Let's go home, daddy." I said sweetly as I pushed back my chair. Tom narrowed his eyes. He was not amused. He handed the waiter seven ones, a ten, and a twenty and stood up.

"After you, Joy," he said.

I walked out of the restaurant with a defiant sway to my hips. The wine was settling into my system quite nicely, and the approving smiles from several men as I walked past their tables added to the glow.

We traveled to the car without speaking. He opened the door. I lowered myself into the seat and asked: "Where to?"

"My apartment?"

"Perfect choice," the wine and I replied.

CHAPTER 29

"What a thoroughly mundane place," I said. "They don't go all out for lodging on temporary placements, do they?"

Tom was hanging his jacket in the hall closet and answered with something that sounded like a snort.

I walked from living room to kitchen and back. As I returned to the main room I stole a quick glance into his bedroom.

"Did you decorate it yourself? Odd choice of artwork," I said pointing to the framed prints of Ecuadorian fishing spiders. Their faces were intriguing; each of the hairy little creatures appeared to be wearing a gray turban and beard; and I could have sworn they had two hands, each encased in a tiny white work glove.

"Ghastly creatures," I said shivering.

"Some astrologers consider the Arachnid the lost thirteenth sign of the zodiac," he replied. "These two are fishing spiders. Fascinating habits actually."

"Well aren't you full of information. Must go over big on a first date."

He ignored my sarcasm. "How about some coffee?" he asked.

"How about a glass of wine?" I countered.

"The last thing you need is wine."

"Well unfortunately, wine is the first thing I want. Will you pour me a glass, or would you prefer I call a cab and go in hunt of some?"

He shook his head and walked to the kitchen. I heard him rummaging in the refrigerator.

"Will red do?" he asked.

I stood in the doorway and watched him pull two glasses from the cupboard. Dick's little sex machine is right, I thought, Tom has an incredible butt.

"Red will be perfect. Thanks. You're an angel." I smiled at my joke. He did not.

I stuck my lower lip out in a fairly decent imitation of Kelly's best pout. "You were more fun as Ted," I said.

"Big deal. I was Mr. Funny and you married Dick, whose sense of humor was largely based upon knock-knock jokes." He handed me a glass of Merlot and refused to meet my eyes.

I stepped back and sipped the wine. "Nice," I said. "Now how about some soft romantic music?"

"Where are you headed with this, Bea or Joy or whoever the hell you think you are right now?"

"I don't know, Ted or Tom, or whoever the hell you think you are," I shot back. "I don't know much of anything anymore!"

I watched his anger drain. His face lost the scowl he'd worn since the restaurant, his shoulders relaxed, and he leaned against the wall. As he sipped his wine, I studied his features. Tom's hair was close enough to Ted's in color if not in texture to be comfortably familiar; but the eyes were nothing like Ted's dark brown orbs, eyes so dark they bordered on black.

"The hardest part of accepting that it is you is the eyes," I said. "Eyes are supposed to be the windows to our souls. Don't get me wrong, those are gorgeous baby blues, but I miss Ted's eyes. If your eyes are different can the soul be yours?"

"It is indeed just a weary old soul in a young body; both unfortunately consumed by the same overwhelming desire."

His voice caressed my skin. Goosebumps dotted my arms as each downy strand of hair strained forward, an invitation to be touched. A barely audible sound escaped my throat. I moved toward him. He took the wine glass from my hand, set it beside his on the counter, and wrapped his arms around me.

"Oh, Bea," he whispered and for once I knew what it meant.

His right hand slid upwards from the nape of my neck into my hair, and he gently traced my ear and stroked the strands of hair that fell free of my hair clip. His other hand followed the curve of my shoulder blade, slowly, intimately, purposely, a blind man's expedition.

I pulled away just enough to see his face. "I can't do this," I said.

"Then don't," he replied. He moved his hand from the hair behind my left ear to my left cheek and traced the pathway tears flow. With the fleshy part of his index finger he brushed my lips before continuing in a direct journey from upper lip to tip of nose to forehead. There he spread his fingers apart and as lightly as a whispered prayer his fingers moved idly down my face, gently closing the lids of my eyes as they passed by.

"I truly don't think I can do this," I protested.

"Then don't," he softly replied. His right hand continued its magic under my chin, butterfly wings flickering against my throat. His left hand moved to a place just below my waist and started a deliberate voyage upward, drawing little circles as he progressed, his touch gentle but undeniably present.

"I don't think I..."

He leaned forward and kissed each eye, the lids still closed. His voice was husky with desire, but calm. "Hush. I will never take what you do not freely give," he said as his lips moved from left eyelid to right.

I stretched to tip toe, my face against his. I wanted to inhale the scent of his skin. I wanted to know the taste of his mouth, to feel the coolness of his teeth against my tongue.

"One kiss," I murmured. "One kiss for old time's sake."

He laughed softly. "The last time you demanded one kiss for old time's sake, a truck destroyed my brand new car and both of us in the process. Are you sure you want to risk that again?"

A sound answered him, a sound that has no name but means come here, come now. My body would know his and my brain could go to hell.

CHAPTER 30

My mother's life was defined by idioms, adages her roadmap for an existence worthy of God's indulgence. She tempered emotions and charted her path guided by the wit and wisdom of the authors of such pearls as: Look before you leap; beggars can't be choosers; and you can't judge a book by its cover.

My sisters and I stumbled through childhood and adolescence, plagued by repetitive exposure to mom's favorite sayings and swore we would never repeat any of them once we left home. That evening as I followed Tom into his bedroom, I rummaged frantically through memories long discarded, longing for some gem to help me through the night.

My behavior mystified me. This surrealistic journey back to the land of the living was undertaken to reclaim the love of my husband. Why then did I crave sex with a body that existed solely as a container for the mystical essence of an old boyfriend? Was my love for Dick fading? Had I fallen in love with Ted's spirit? Or was I simply lusting for Tom's youthful body?

Tom did not appear to be wrestling with such weighty issues. His dress shirt was off, tossed carelessly onto the floor;

and he was balanced precariously on one leg, the other struggling to be free of his jeans.

"Can I help you shed that sweater?" he asked.

His attitude annoyed me. I wanted to come to judgment not orgasm. Unfortunately, I also wanted to touch him and I was especially interested in the areas that disappeared into the legs of his boxers. I could feel the warmth of a blush moving from neck to cheeks as my mind raced with ambivalence, a dead giveaway to my angst. Ted's face appeared as serenely pale as it had moments before. Obviously blood was rushing to a different part of his body.

"You know," I said in a frantic attempt to gain control of my galloping libido, "for someone so damned evolved your restraint is far from impressive."

"Ah, yes, evolution," he purred. "Species evolve, but without sexual attraction, the natural process of reproduction wouldn't have a chance." He smiled without embarrassment at his inane babbling, and raised one eyebrow, as if to say: Don't you agree?

I rolled my eyes and shook my head in disgust.

"Yup, me too," he said, then he lifted his T-shirt and with a careless toss it too adorned the floor.

I groaned. The hairs on my neck danced to the husky, sensual music of his voice and the glorious sight of his nearly naked body. Be strong, some part of my mind screamed. I struggled valiantly to exude resolve or at least to postpone the inevitable.

I made one final attempt at control. "If I were you," I said, "I would worry about how this is playing in Clarence's little corner of the universe. Perhaps the angelic tribunal is, at this very moment, watching us and slating you for return as a slug."

He smiled. "Could happen, I suppose, but if so, maybe I can talk them into a co-reincarnation. I can see it now: just you and me, two happy slugs, sliding along through life together. That sounds pretty damn good, although I doubt I will be very popular with the other slugs, if they get wind of my current vocation."

I fought the smile that was threatening to disrupt my righteous anger. "Seriously, Tom, I know I said I wanted a kiss..."

"That you did," he replied. He moved closer.

"And I did want to kiss you. Do want to kiss you," I added.

"Well then?" The space between us had all but disappeared. My ability to think rationally was quickly following suit.

I tried once more. "But what if it is wrong for us to do this?"

"Then you will be returned to the same level from which you arrived at level twenty-five, and I will be a slug with the most satisfied grin ever sported by man or bug."

His fingers moved to my sweater, and I could feel the top button slowly begin to surrender to his will. I pushed his hands away.

"Some things are not meant to happen at the pace of the slug," I murmured as I hurriedly undid each circular pearl button.

Slipping my arms free of the sweater, I moved my face to his. My lips kissed the tip of his chin and quickly moved to his mouth. There was within me a symphony of emotion: the passion of youthful exploration; the forbidden fruit of bodies unexplored; a fierceness of tempo uncontrolled by expectations past or future; and yet quietly, insistently a rhythm of two souls familiar and intertwined.

I sensed rather than felt his hands as they moved with soft caress and gentle demand over my arms and back, down to each fingertip and up into each tiny curve. His exploration finished he journeyed to my shoulders and down each arching blade. Confident fingers unhooked my bra, and edged the straps off to the side, allowing his fingertips to softly tease the skin beneath his touch.

Little sounds of pleasure proclaimed my reaction as his hands moved from my back and slowly circled each breast. His kisses, at first tender and playful became more demanding. His touch secure, he explored with hands and mouth until my skin raged hot against his, and I burned with the very want of him. His body pressed against my own, he guided me gently towards the bed.

"Are you sure you can do this?" he whispered.

No words were needed. My body answered with delight.

CHAPTER 31

He was standing at the stove as I emerged from the bathroom. "Hi beautiful," he said, seemingly intent upon organizing his supplies and utensils. I knew better. Finally he turned to face me.

"I thought I'd make ham and cheese omelets but I could do pancakes if you would prefer. I make terrific pancakes. So, which will it be, my love? Pancakes or omelet or both?"

I could taste the anxiety in his light-hearted query. I knew the words he hoped to hear and what he feared, and as much as I hated to upset him, I knew I would.

"I'm late for work," I answered. "If the future Mrs. McBane gets annoyed with me I could lose my job; and then this nearly hopeless situation I am in will be impossible."

As I spoke, I slipped on a navy cardigan; still amazed by the breasts that held my blouse away from my body and the long shapely legs that propelled me from place to place. I wiggled slightly, enjoying the luscious curves and the fit of my slacks.

"So your quest for revenge remains unchanged by what happened between us last night? That's really too bad, Joy. I had hoped you might have awakened with a different goal." He turned his back to me and poured coffee into a green stoneware mug. His words hung between us.

"Don't be mad," I pleaded. "You know I'm trying to save my marriage."

He turned at that, funeral eyes warning that civility had just been abandoned.

"Damn it! There is no marriage to save. You are not Bea."

"So you say, but that doesn't make it so! My heart is hers. The pain, the jealousy, the anger, hers – all hers! Other than the absence of a flat-chested over-weight body, I am Bea!"

He slammed his mug down on the counter. The glass shattered, splattering hot brown liquid from counter to floor. He extended his right arm toward me, one rigid finger slicing the air as it journeyed to its destination, inches from my face.

"You are not Bea!" he shouted. "Bea is dead, gone, finished as a mortal being. She cannot be resurrected. Her spirit still lives, but even that spirit will not be Bea's in a short time."

Tears filled my eyes and I stood silent against the assault.

Tom sighed. "You are not Bea." His final words shouted in a whisper, he closed the distance between us, his breath caressing my face.

"I can accept that your love for Dick has survived the grave. I can accept that what happened between us last night was nothing more than a combination of too much wine and the youthful lust of the bodies we're using..." His voice betrayed his pain.

"Not just that, Ted," I whispered.

"Tom," he reminded me.

"Tom," I replied. "Not just what you said. Not just wine and lust!"

"Okay, not only that. But whatever it was, it was not what I'd hoped, and in any event, it was not enough to change your mind. I accept that, but please try to understand the futility of your mission. You have two weeks left to do what you will do, and you just might wreck Mercedes' relationship with Dick, but even if you do, you cannot take her place. That will never be allowed. Revenge is an option. Being Dick's wife is not."

His words struck my body, forcing all the air from my lungs.

"Oh, Tom, what if I can't even do that..."

"What if you can't even do what?"

"What if I fail to wreck Mercedes' hold on Dick? What if I die or get recalled or however the hell this dumb-assed procedure works and my last conscious thought is that he still loves her?"

The sobs came then, the sobs that did not come when they should have, the day I found the package in Dick's gym bag, the day my heart shattered into a thousand meandering pieces.

A hand touched my face. Gentle fingers wiped the tears that dripped.

"Oh, Bea," he said, and he opened his arms.

I ached to be held, but I lifted my chin in defiance and turned my face from his. I could not forgive his words.

"Why should I expect you to support me?" I asked. "You don't understand how it feels when the person you love loves someone else!" As soon as the words were spoken I shuddered. "I'm sorry," I said, risking a glance in his direction.

His arms remained open and inviting. His face gave no evidence of anger or of pain. "Come here precious girl," he commanded. "Everything will be okay. I promise."

This time I obeyed. I leaned against him then, my words whispered but intense: "How will everything be all right? Tell me how."

He leaned back and looked into my eyes. "Plan A: You seduce Dick," he said. "You greet him when he comes home dressed in shorts and a blouse. I suggest you leave one button open. You might dose your head under the shower to achieve that neat droplet of water meandering toward a breast effect. That should get his attention. It certainly worked with me."

I laughed at the memory. His face remained serious. My laughter stopped. "I can't do that," I said. "I would feel dirty if I used Joy's body to seduce Dick." I locked onto his eyes, willing him to understand my seemingly foolish moral dilemma.

"Yeah, I figured that," he said. "Which brings us to Plan B."

"Plan B?"

"Yup. Plan B."

"Should I ask?"

He paused. To reconsider? For emphasis? Finally he spoke. "You want Mercedes and Dick's relationship to end."

I shook my head yes.

"Do you care how it ends?"

"What do you mean?" I asked.

"Just what I said. Do you care *how* it ends? In other words, does Dick have to be the one to put a bullet in it for you to be happy?"

"I wish he would end it, sure, but I wasn't born yesterday. Well actually I guess I was born yesterday, but you know what I mean. So the answer is: I want it ended in whatever way that can happen. But if Dick doesn't pull the plug, who will? Merci sure as hell isn't going to. She has everything she wants now. Why would she walk away from that?"

"Because she likes my sexy little butt. I heard her tell you that." He smiled. He looked so satisfied that I hated to ruin his dream, but I did not have time to humor delusions.

"Sexy little butt aside, Tom, Merci isn't going to dump her Sugar Daddy to date the Bug-Be-Gone man."

"I know that, silly girl. I'm not as dumb as you think, despite the fact that I too was born yesterday. I figure Merci just might date a Bug-Be-Gone Man who is running away from his demanding-but-oh-so-wealthy father." His smile screamed self-satisfaction.

"You would do that?"

"I would do anything for you if I thought it would make you happy. I told you that a long time ago," he said. "So go on back to doing what you have to do, Joy. I'll do the same."

He turned and walked into the bedroom. The door he closed behind him was an ordinary door, a hollow slab of pressed wood, yet it seemed a portage impenetrable, a distance too far to circumvent. I swallowed emotions that surged unbidden and walked out of his apartment.

CHAPTER 32

"Sorry!" I followed my shouted apology through the back door, and faced my employer's lover armed with multiple excuses for being late. None were needed.

Mercedes glanced up briefly from her chair at the kitchen table, then returned her gaze to the still wet polish on her nails.

"What do you think of this color?" she asked. "I liked it when I saw it in *Marie Claire*, but now that I have it on, it looks too prissy and maidenly. I prefer a sexier look. Here you take it." She stood up and offered the bottle of OPI polish with a sweet smile that failed to compensate for the implication behind her gift.

"Pink is not my shade either. Why not give it to Kelly?" I said.

"Oh, pul-lease. You can't be serious. Dick is barely able to handle the fact that Kelly is getting her ears pierced sooner than her mother had decreed. He seems so nervous about that decision that I swear he thinks Beatrice is watching from the great beyond." She laughed at that, irritating shotgun laughter, the nasal sounds punctuated by alternating sharp intakes of air.

"Maybe she is," I replied.

"Good Lord, Joy, I hope you aren't serious. You are too bright for that kind of religious pabulum, and Dick won't want a religious zealot watching his kids." She sucked her bottom lip inward and shook her head as if observing a delinquent student.

"I wasn't speaking literally," I said. "After all I..."

Her hand waved me silent. "Never mind," she said. "I need to let you get to work. I didn't do anything with the beds or dishes. I figured you have your own ways."

"Yes, thank you, Ma'am," I answered.

"Oh, good gracious Joy, I hate being called Ma'am."

"Sorry, Ma'am, I mean Merci. My parents taught me to be respectful to anyone older than me." I could barely restrain the corners of my mouth at her obvious displeasure.

"I hardly qualify as older," she snapped.

I smiled as I removed my cardigan and stretched, aware that her eyes were focused upon my perfect chest. Her horrified expression was a much better a reaction to my voluptuous form than I hoped however, and the exclamation that followed was truly mystifying.

"Ants!" She spit the word at me.

"Excuse me?" I said, glancing fearfully down at my breasts.

"No, not on you. There!" She raised her arm and gestured frantically at the table behind us, where remnants of Ben and Kelly's breakfast were covered by thousands of happy little bugs.

"Oh yuk, they make my skin crawl. I was just sitting there," she added, brushing her arms as she backed away.

I turned my face from her view and rolled my eyes. Act One, Invasion of the Ants, I thought. "Shall I call the exterminating service that was here the other day?" I asked in as servile a tone as I could manage.

"You bet and tell them they better cover this under the warranty."

I opened the drawer in the cabinet to the left of the wall phone and searched for the BUGS BE GONE phone number.

"Found their card," I announced. I dialed, expecting to hear Tom's voice on the other end, since this was obviously his show. Instead a voice of undeniably Bronx origin answered: "Welcome to Bugs Be Gone Exterminators. How shall I direct your call?"

I looked at the card again. Could I have been wrong? Could this be simply what it seems, a persistent colony of ants? "I'm calling from the McBane home, 110 Basil Drive," I said. "One of your employees, a Tom Gardengle, sprayed for ants yesterday and we have a major swarm of them in the kitchen this morning."

There was a pause. "Hold on," the voice commanded.

I waited. "I'm on hold," I explained to Merci's hissed demand to know what was happening.

Nasal-twang returned. "Okie-dokie. Mr. Gardengle is in your neighborhood and can arrive within thirty minutes. Will someone be there to let him in the house?"

"Someone will," I replied. I lowered the phone to the cradle. These ants were not just a coincidence, I decided. This was definitely Tom's doing, and it should be fun to watch.

"The fellow who was here yesterday is in the neighborhood and they said he can be here within thirty minutes," I said.

"The cute guy with the sexy butt?"

I nodded.

"God he was hot! Humm, think I just might stay around long enough to let him in. I wouldn't mind replacing the image of those disgusting insects with the sight of his tight little behind." Merci smiled, pulled a comb and lipstick from her purse and turned toward the powder room. "Go on upstairs and get started on the beds. I'll listen for the door."

"Yell if you need me," I said.

I wish Dick could hear his precious little trophy talk shamelessly about ogling an exterminator's butt, I thought, as I took a stab at the mess Merci had left on the stove. Then I moved to the family room and gathered all the paraphernalia that the kids had left in their typical morning madness. Finally I started up the steps. The doorbell buzzed before I reached midpoint. I stopped and listened.

Mercedes' stilettos clicked-clacked to the front door.

"Hey, gorgeous," a strong seductive voice rang out. "I hear you have some nasty little crawly creatures." He whistled softly. "And I can see right off why you have a problem."

"You can? From the front door?"

"Yup. Ants like sweet things and you sure are one sweet thing."

Good Lord! Bug-be-Gone Man sounded like a junior high school Romeo. So much for Plan B. I might as well grab a can of Raid and go on down to clean up the damn ants myself, I thought.

"You sure are one sweet thing..." I muttered to myself as I turned to start back down the steps. "Men are such idiots. No one would fall for that crap."

Her voice stopped me.

"Would you like something cold to drink?" The question was followed by a nervous giggle. I stood suspended, my right foot inches from the bottom step.

"How about I give the ants the old heave ho and then we both have something cold. Maybe a beer?"

"Sounds good to me, but can you do that? Drink on the job that is. What if your boss finds out?"

Now I couldn't see into the kitchen from my spot on the second step, but I was willing to bet that actual sap was dripping from Merci's mouth. Better not get too close to the ants, I thought.

"Hey, no worries. Even if I needed the job, which I don't, it would be worth the risk to spend the afternoon with someone as gorgeous as you."

Now you have gone too far, I thought. Even shallow woman will see through that line. I waited for her dismissive reply. It would be a long wait.

"You aren't too bad to look at yourself." The words oozed out of her mouth...sticky syrupy glob-covered words. Drip, drip, drip, splat. Sap. Definitely sap.

"Still you really shouldn't take chances," she continued. "I mean this is your source of income. Unless you are independently wealthy..." She laughed. "I guess there isn't much chance of that, because then why would you be doing this job in the first place."

"Well, pretty woman, funny you should mention that, because rolling in money is exactly what I am. So stop worrying about my employment status and fetch us a beer while I decrease the ant population by a few hundred of its finest."

"You're rolling in money?" I could hear the disbelief in her voice. "You are handing me a line."

"Not at all. I am handing you the truth, sweetheart, the truth, the whole truth and nothing but the truth." he laughed, a deep-throated Marlborough Man laugh. "I have more money than you have sex appeal and believe me, sweet thing, that is more than anyone needs."

He paused. Did he flex a muscle, or perhaps conger up a black American Express card? I slid one foot to the hardwood floor and dared a peek around the corner. Her back was to the doorway. His eyes were fixed upon her, his gaze adoring.

I couldn't see her face but her body language screamed: "Take me!" She leaned toward Ted, one hand seductively intertwined in her hair, the other resting on her thigh, fingers arched, fingertips moving ever so slowly, a slow scratch of a sensuous itch.

I willed Ted to look at me. No such luck. He seemed completely unaware of my presence. I waved one hand over my head. No reaction. His eyelids were slightly closed, the proverbial bedroom eyes effect. I raised my middle finger in the air and glared at him. Still he ignored me. He studied her features with complete absorption.

Damn him! He was either an exceptionally good actor or Dick's little seductress had just captured the attention of the only other man I'd ever loved.

As I was contemplating the possibility of throwing a shoe at the back of Merci's head, Ted reached out his hands and slid his fingers across her shoulders until they met at the center of her back. He moved closer and finally spoke.

"I took this job to prove a point to my dad," he said, "and maybe just to annoy old money bags a bit in the process, but there comes a time..." he let his voice drop off.

He waited, his line in the water, the bait flopping helplessly back and forth. He made no movement to alert his target to the danger that accompanied the banquet. The seconds ticked away.

She bit.

"Regular beer or Lite?"

"Regular." He whacked his hard stomach for emphasis and smiled. "And maybe you can put some music on for round two."

She tilted her head and nuzzled his outstretched arm. "I probably shouldn't be drinking a first round of beer let alone a second. It isn't even noon yet," she purred.

"Who said round two had anything to do with beer?"

I heard bug man laugh low and warm, and a female voice reply so softly that the words were indistinguishable. I swallowed emotions I could not identify, pivoted and walked quickly up the stairs. There was an awful lot I did not understand, but of one thing I was suddenly certain: I did not want to be here when Plan B evolved.

CHAPTER 33

It took less than five minutes to make the bed in the master bedroom, a bed that would, I guessed, be unmade shortly. Now I simply had to find a way to convince Dick to come home mid-morning, not an easy task on a school day.

What should I tell him? Let's see, I thought, as I slowly walked back down the stairs, I could say the roof is leaking, or maybe the pipes have burst, or the television exploded, or my personal favorite: Best hurry home, Dick, your lover is doing the horizontal dance with the exterminator.

"I've got to run some errands. I'll be gone for a couple hours," I yelled in the direction of the kitchen as I grabbed my jacket and keys.

Merci's head appeared around the corner. Her cheeks were flushed. "Take your time, Joy," she purred. "Buy yourself some lunch and relax a bit. All work and no play as they say..."

"Do you want me to clean up the kitchen before I leave?" I started to move toward her.

"No!" She moved to block the doorway.

"Seriously," she said, her voice calmer as I backed away, "don't worry about things here. You do your errands and have a nice long lunch. Maybe even get your hair done. You could use a day of pampering. You are such a hard worker." Drip. Drip. Drip. Sap is flowing once again.

"Gee thanks, that sounds wonderful," I said suppressing a gag. I flashed my jack-o-lantern smile and left.

Twenty minutes later I arrived at the high school and parked in the same spot I always did. An appreciative whistle greeted my exit from the car.

"Do you know where I can find Coach McBane?" I asked the young man who stood before me.

"Well she-it," he declared with enthusiasm. "You're the nanny, are you? I heard you were hot, but I never would have dreamed you were this hot! She-it you're fine!"

"Yes, well, thank you, I guess," I stammered, "So if you could just point me in the direction of your coach?"

"Hey, why bother with the old guy? How about you come over to my place and let me point you in the direction of some real fun." He thrust his pelvis forward, just in case I missed his ever so subtle innuendo.

"I need to see Coach McBane," I said in as firm a tone as I could manage. "Save the sex talk. I couldn't be less interested. I want directions and nothing else. Point if you can't talk without making an ass of yourself."

"Well fuck you," he said as he pivoted and stomped away.

"Hey!" I yelled. "Just point, damn it!"

He did.

CHAPTER 34

I found Dick in the gymnasium. He was leaning against the wall, clipboard in hand. He waved me in, and I watched him flash an encouraging smile to each kid who jogged past him.

"Can I talk with you a minute?" I asked.

"Of course," he said and yelled to the kids: "Three more laps around the gym and then break into pairs for sit-ups. I'll be right outside the door. No lagging behind."

Dick's smile faded as I poured out my tale.

"You are sure about what you saw?" he asked, his lips tight, his voice restrained.

"Yes, sir, I am. I'm sorry." I said. "The exterminator got there just as I was going to run some errands. I said I could go later, but Merci said to go. She said I should take my time and even stop for lunch if I wanted, that she would stay until he left. I thought that was nice of her, but I didn't want to take advantage, so I came back pretty quickly.

When I got inside I heard some sounds from the second floor so I figured he was spraying up there too. But when I walked past your bedroom the door was partway open and I saw them on the bed. They were naked and I was so embarrassed that I didn't even say anything. I just ran out of the house, and then I came here."

I watched him swallow.

"The thing is, sir, I don't think I can keep on working for you. I feel so awful about deserting the kids and all, but I have no experience with stuff like this."

"You're quitting?"

"Yes sir. That's why I had to come here. I mean I couldn't just disappear and not even say goodbye to Ben and Kelly, but what do I tell them? I was already having trouble knowing what to say to Kelly. She was upset about Merci being there overnight. She said she knew what you were doing and I did not have a clue about how to answer that. And now this... I didn't know what else to do except to come and tell you, but you seem so upset. Maybe I shouldn't have come..."

"No, no. You did the right thing." He shivered and rubbed his right hand vigorously up and down his left arm.

I hadn't expected him to be this shaken. I reached out and gently touched his arm.

"I'm really sorry, Mr. McBane," I said.

Dick's shoulders dropped. His eyes fill with tears, and I frowned as his face hardened against the pain of her betrayal.

What's good for the goose is be good for the gander, I thought. Then how come right now it does not feel all that good? A familiar emotion started to bubble up from deep within my gut. I recognized it immediately. It was guilt, authentic hard-core guilt, guilt passed down from generation to generation, guilt so strong that it survived my transformation into a different human being.

"I am so very sorry," I whispered. "I never should have told you."

"S'okay," he said, as he swiped at the tears. "Look, Joy, I don't know what to say. I'm pretty devastated, and I'm sorry you had to see something like that. I don't blame you for wanting to quit, but I hope you will stay. I think the kids need you. I know I need you."

My heart beat to the rhythm of love reclaimed. Blood rushed joyously to my face. Dick needed me! Ted was wrong. Dick could sense that I was more than a nanny. I moved toward him, expecting his arms to open in welcome.

"Of course I will stay," I said soothingly.

"Thank you," he said.

His arms remained tightly at his side. I retreated back a step.

"This means a lot," he said. "I could not have handled having to start the whole nanny search all over again. Not now. Not with this happening."

I backed further away, my face flaming with shame. How could I have been so stupid! There was no cosmic connection. Dick needed my services not me. I struggled for composure. Guilt faded under the superior power of anger.

Suddenly Dick moved into the space I'd vacated. He patted me on the shoulder. "You cannot know how much I appreciate this, Joy. Of course I will give you a raise for staying and I can promise you that you won't have to deal with anything like that again."

"How can you promise that?" I asked, bitterness hardening my voice.

"Because after school I'll let Mercedes know she is no longer welcome in my house."

"And what about in your heart, Dick? Is she welcome there?" My words surprised me. I had not intended to speak them.

Dick stiffened. "That's an oddly personal question for you to ask me, Joy, but you did, and I understand how hard this has been for you, so I'll answer." As he stood silent, his eyes wandered from the clock on the opposite wall, to the water fountain, to the pile of backpacks and gym bags on the floor outside the door to the gym as if one of them might hold answers. Finally he sighed, swallowed, and spoke. His voice was quiet and deadly. His eyes flashed anger and determination: "I will let Merci know that there is no place for her in my heart."

He shook his head, and in a voice so quiet I had to strain to hear, he said to no one but himself, "Fuck it all. I guess I deserve this. Maybe this is what happens when a person screws up as badly as I did."

"I don't understand," I said, although I did.

He startled, perhaps surprised that I heard him. "No," he mumbled. "Of course not."

"I'd like to," I whispered.

He stood immobile, his face unreadable, his body language no more help. Finally, just as I was about to tell him to never mind, he answered.

"I had a wife who loved me," he said, "but I wanted something more, something..." He sighed and rubbed his hand across his forehead.

I leaned a little closer. "You wanted something..." I repeated softly.

He looked into my eyes, an unflinching stare. For a moment I thought he recognized me, and then he looked away.

"You're young. You must know that glorious emotion that comes with falling in love," he said. "The sweet ache that crawls under your skin and makes you lie awake, wanting the other person, tasting them in the wine you drink, feeling them in the mist of the morning air? Well someone came into my life and said things that I hadn't heard in so many years, things that made that glorious emotion come alive. Pretty soon she was all I could think about..."

"Mercedes?" I asked.

"Yes," he answered. "Mercedes."

"For a while life seemed as perfect as life can be," he said. "I felt like a teenager in love. I even bought into the stupid rationale that it could not be wrong if it felt so good." He made a sound in his throat.

I nodded but did not risk speaking.

"But then Beanie found out. Her friends called her that," he added in explanation, "I think that nickname bothered her sometimes. She thought she was too small, up here you know." He pointed to his chest. "That was what she thought, but she was just about perfect."

I saw a smile cross his face, in an instant there and gone. I heard him sigh again.

"After Bea found out about Mercedes, and before I was able to make myself end things with Merci, Bea was killed in an accident." He lowered his head and pulled his lips inward as if to keep control.

"Jane said it happened out near your lake house," I said.

"Yes, a few miles from there. We were having a party for Bea's 25th high school reunion. I had gone up to the bedroom to make a call to Merci, and I think Bea heard it. She didn't say anything, but I'm pretty sure that's what happened, because right after that, she left the party with her high school boyfriend."

Once more he retreated into silence. This time I waited without comment.

"She came out of the house right after I did, and she was different."

"Different?"

"Her hair, her face, I don't know. Something. Anyway she left with Ted and their car was hit by a truck that had lost its brakes and they were both killed instantly. I always wonder if she got even with me before the accident, if she..." His voice wavered. Tears rolled down his face.

"No she didn't!" I exclaimed without thinking.

Thunder roared.

"I mean I've heard Jane and Lorna talk about what happened. They said the accident happened not that far from the house and hardly any time after they left. I don't see how anything could have happened." I waited nervously. No angry angel came for me and I breathed my relief.

"Yeah, I know," he said. "I went a little crazy for a while and alienated Bea's folks, probably forever, with some of the things I said, but all along I knew she wasn't doing anything except getting away from my stupid behavior." He straightened and wiped his eyes.

"Anyway, I lost Bea and for what? Merci obviously doesn't love me. So tonight I will send her away. I should have done it a long time ago."

Suddenly he slapped one hand against his leg. "Oh hell," he said, "there is no point in putting off confronting her until after school. I am going to find someone to cover my classes for me and do it now."

"Now?"

"Yes. Why wait?"

"Well, why hurry? I mean do you want to make a scene? Why not wait until you've calmed down? Maybe there's an explanation."

I could not believe I said that! My mouth seemed to have a mind of its own. Everything is progressing exactly according to plan and all I have to do is shut up and let it happen. What is wrong with me?

Dick stared at me but did not answer.

"I mean, what are you going to do now that you couldn't do later?" I asked quietly.

"You ask the oddest questions. What am I going to do now?" He snorted his displeasure. "Nothing too dramatic; just toss the little tramp out and make sure she doesn't give me, or you, any more trouble. Could I do it later? Sure. But why wait. There aren't any explanations I need to hear."

"But I don't see why. I mean I..."

"Joy, I know what I'm doing. Don't give me any grief on this. I have had all the grief I can handle." He shook his head. "I could use a ride though. It'll give me time to pull myself together. I'll meet you in at the parking lot in fifteen."

He waved me away and walked toward the gym.

As I watched him, I felt strangely depressed. I should be ecstatic, I thought. After all, I planted the seeds and tended the field and my crop is about to harvest. So what the hell is wrong with me?

"Dick!" I yelled.

He turned around.

"I've to go. You'll have to drive yourself." I turned and ran toward my car before he could react.

Damn it Clarence, I thought, why this? Why now?

CHAPTER 35

I arrived at the house in half the usual driving time.

"Ted," I screamed as I rushed into the master bedroom without knocking, "I can't do it!"

Two naked bodies unraveled.

"What the hell? And who's Ted?" Mercedes flashed me a look of fury.

Ted smiled and pumped his fist in a motion of victory.

"You know what this will mean?" he asked.

"Yes," I whispered.

"Are you sure? There won't be another chance."

"I'm sure," I said.

I turned to Merci. "Listen up," I said, fighting the emotions that threatened to surface at the sight of her perfect body. "You've been set up. Dick is on his way home."

She gasped. "You little bitch," she hissed.

"Yeah, well no more so than you were," I replied quietly. "But you get a gift that Beatrice didn't. You get a chance to save your relationship with Dick. So here's what I think we have to do." I explained as quickly as possible.

Mercedes looked at me with contempt. "You're fucking crazy!" she screamed at me. "I sure as hell am not going to do any of that!"

Ted touched her on the shoulder. She turned and looked into his eyes. She listened as he spoke, quietly and firmly. He could not tell her the truth of who we were, but his version of reality was enough to convince Mercedes. Finally she sighed heavily and nodded her acquiescence.

The sight of the two of them stark naked and face-to-face was unnerving. "Time is passing!" I yelled.

Merci grabbed her clothes. "Do it," she said.

Ted slapped her across the face, hard enough to leave a handprint. A trickle of blood dribbled from one corner of her mouth.

"Now go turn on the shower and sit on the floor in the corner of the stall. He'll hear the shower and find you there. You know what to say."

Merci shook her head, bit her lip against the pain, and ran into the bathroom.

I yanked the covers off of the bed as Ted dressed, turned over a chair, and swept the photographs onto the floor. Each noise tore into my heart. I knew what had to come next. My quest for revenge had ended and Dick was gone from my life. But in a moment I needed to let go of another person, and I knew that this time we would say goodbye forever.

Ted moved toward me calmly but purposefully. He raised one hand and gently caressed my face. "No sorrow," he whispered. "You will always be a part of me; a flicker of a smile, a shiver in the darkness, a teardrop. I may not remember your name or your face, but I will love you forever Beatrice Marie Kelly McBane."

With those words he walked out of the room and out of my life.

I grabbed the phone and dialed 9-1-1.

"Send an ambulance!" I screamed into the phone. "I think the woman I work for has been raped!"

CHAPTER 36

"How was school?" I asked without turning around as the door slammed.

"Great!"

Kelly skipped across the kitchen and hugged me. "Dad said Merci is feeling better today and that we are all going out for Chinese. You too, Joy."

"Maybe," I said.

"You have to come with us. Don't say 'maybe' cause grown-ups always mean no when they say maybe." she stomped her foot for emphasis. "Merci will be upset if you don't come. Dad said you are her hero, that you saved her life."

"Kelly, I keep telling you that is not true. The man was already gone when I got here. I simply called 9-1-1. Please stop making more of what I did, than actually happened."

"Well, I don't care! I think you saved her." She smiled and wiggled her body, arms folded in front of her waist. "Do not try to resist. Ve have vays to make you go to dinner," she said laughing.

The phone rang and she lunged to grab it – a perfect preteen maneuver. "Hello?"

"It's for you," she said as she handed me the phone, her voice dripping with disappointment.

"Cheer up, sweetie," I soothed. "Soon it will be ringing off the hook for you."

I raised the phone to my ear. "Hello?"

"It's time," a familiar voice intoned.

I turned to the wall, my back to Kelly.

"Not now," I whispered. "Please not so soon." I could feel the panic begin. There was no reply.

"What do I say?" I asked with resignation.

"You will know," the voice replied.

I carefully placed the receiver on the hook and turned just as Ben and Dick rushed in from the garage.

"God, I'm starving! Did Kelly tell you we are all going out for Chinese tonight?" Dick asked, tossing his briefcase on the table and heading for the refrigerator.

"I can't," I said.

"Someone called," Kelly said. Her voice was somber, her eyes sad. "Joy got upset."

Dick stopped rummaging in the refrigerator and turned. "What's up?" he asked.

"My aunt is very ill. I have to go and take care of her. I have to leave this afternoon. It probably will be long-term. You better not plan on me coming back." I could feel the words clump into a ball in my throat.

Kelly began to cry. Ben threw his backpack on the floor and stomped out of the room.

"Can't you stay a little while?" Dick asked. "Maybe just until I find someone to help with the kids?"

"No. I have to go now. They've already booked me on a flight. I'm so sorry."

"The kids need you," he said.

I struggled without success to keep from crying. "I am sure Merci will help out until you find someone and Lorna and Jane are always willing to help. And don't forget to ask my – I mean Kelly and Ben's grandma and grandpa."

He shrugged his shoulders. "They don't really want to talk to me," he said.

"I know they were pretty angry with you," I replied, "but they love the kids and they will forgive you. You have to be the one to ask, though, Dick. You have to be the one to say you are sorry, to them, to Lorna and to Jane too. That's the only way to heal the hurt."

"I'll make the effort, Joy. I'll mend the fences. I promise," he said as if it were normal for us to talk of such things. "I promise to do all those things you ask, but I still wish you would stay a little while. This is too quick. We really will miss you Joy."

Kelly sobbed, "Please, Joy."

Words failed me. I shook my head no.

Dick put his arm around Kelly and said: "Go call grandma, sweetie. Tell her daddy needs to talk."

I smiled through my tears.

After Kelly left the room, Dick turned to me. "Are you sure, Joy? Is there no one else who could help out with your aunt for a while? Please try to think of someone. We all need you."

I know I answered him. I know we talked and cried and talked some more. I know I packed my clothes and hugged my children and the man, who still felt in my heart like my husband. I know I walked out of my house, suitcase in hand, and that my feet moved left, right, left, right, further and further away from what I finally knew without hesitation could never again be home.

I looked back once, a quick hungry glance. Dick, Ben and Kelly stood melded together. A car passed to my left and pulled to the curb in front of the house, my parents' car. A layer had been mended, a fragile beginning but I had faith that it would hold.

But something was wrong. I could not find my car and a storm was brewing, fierce winds came rushing toward me, blowing so strong I could hardly stand. I turned and yelled back for help. "I can't see," I called. "I cannot find my car! Dick? Mom? Dad? Can anyone hear me?"

Suddenly the storm abated and I could glide through the currents above my house. Voices pulled me and I saw them, tucked into the curve of a raindrop: my mom, Ben and Kelly. They were making cookies and mom was talking, answering questions I could not hear. She smiled as she spoke, flour on her nose, fiercely beating the batter without pause.

"Try to forgive her, Kelly. She had no choice. She had to go."

"I don't care if she does have to take care of some dumb sick old woman. I still wish Joy were here!" Kelly's voice floated up and wrapped around my heart.

"She said she wouldn't even be able to write," Ben added, his voice hard and unforgiving. "Who can't even write a letter? If she loved us, she would."

"Put away the anger, Ben," Mom chided. "Best not to be too quick to judge what's in the hearts of others. Forgiving is hard work, but life requires it. Now let's get these cookies in the oven so we can surprise your dad when he gets home."

I reached an arm toward the three who carried my genes – one as supplier, the other two recipients.

"I love you all," I cried as the darkness claimed me. "I wish you could know that I would have stayed if I could."

CHAPTER 37

"Welcome back, Beatrice." Clarence beamed his approval. "You had us worried for a while, but you did okay. Yes, my dear, you did very well indeed!"

I laughed, a sound I would not have thought possible. I did not feel sorrow. Cautiously, as if for the first time, my eyes met those of the angel standing before me.

"I know," he said with a mammoth smile. "You feel only what you should."

"Clarence?" I searched for words to ask what I knew I should not.

"No, Bea, you cannot see him." He answered my unspoken question without pretense. "Ted has already moved on to his next earthly experience."

"It's okay," I said, even though it really was not. I sniffed back tears and straightened my shoulders. "I just wanted to say goodbye, to tell him I was sorry for being such an idiot most of the time I was Joy."

As the sobs silently exploded deep within me, he continued: "We thought it best that the two of you not be here together. I really am sorry, Beatrice."

"So now what?" I asked in as brave a voice as I could manage. "Do I get plopped back into the infant pool?"

"Only if that is what you want, Beatrice. You earned your placement. You may choose."

"Seriously? I get to be a level twenty-five? I didn't think I would be able to. I wasn't exactly evolved most of the three weeks."

"True," Clarence replied. "But at the end, dear Beatrice, you were all we could wish you to be, and the ending is what counts. It is not a task of canceling out the bad with the good, of accumulating a certain amount of points. No, Beatrice, fair or not, and indeed sometimes it most definitely is not, the decision is based upon what you make of yourself when all is said and done. And you were perfect. So, yes, you may choose."

I stood before him unprepared for the task. Despite his reassurance, I did not feel worthy or evolved.

"So, Bea, what will you do with your next life? Solve a mystery, cure a disease, end world hunger?" He smiled but I knew the question was as serious as I would ever have to answer.

"Well, I don't know, I mean none of what you say," I stammered.

Clarence cleared his angelic throat and commanded: "Beatrice Joy, stop trying to figure out what you should want! Trust what is inside. What does your heart tell you to do with your next life?"

"Okay." I took a deep breath. "I would like to be important in one person's life. I would like to be needed. And, Clarence, if it could happen, I would like to be a mom. Is that too small a wish? Do I disappoint you?"

"No, Bea, you do not."

"I can be someone's mom then? Someone who needs to be loved? You are sure it is not too meaningless a request?"

I looked at Clarence through tears. His blurred image nodded.

"It is often in the ordinary that the miraculous hides," he said. "Your choices are good. Your placement shall be exactly as you wish and I will look forward to meeting you again someday. Good-bye, Beatrice."

"I don't need to go back right away," I said, fear creeping into my heart. "I wouldn't mind staying here a while. You could teach me things. I could be a greeter." I smiled. "I'll miss you, Clarence."

"So rent the movie," he said. "I hear the resemblance is quite amusing." I felt his hand touch my head, a hand far too gentle to belong to an angel of his majesty.

As the storm approached, whirling me from his side, I called out: "How will I know who I am?"

His answer was but a whisper in my ear: "You will know."

PROLOGUE

"Mom, wake up! I'm going to be late for my game if we don't hurry."

My eyes struggled to open. The face before me was contorted with emotion. I had never seen him before, yet I knew him with the same assurance as I knew myself, past and present. Clarence had granted my wish in entirety. I was a mom and I was indeed needed, because I was the only parent this child had. His dad was gone, leaving without a proper explanation or goodbye. Just a note taped to the refrigerator that said he'd gone off to find a better life.

Well Frankie and I will do just fine, I thought. I have so much love to give, love from Ben and Kelly and..." Tears threatened at the memories. I fought the sadness and hopped out of bed.

"Go, get ready. We'll be fine," I instructed him.

As soon as he left I lifted my nightgown over my head. "Well shoot," I mumbled as I caught sight of my new body in the mirror. "Not much there to speak of!"

As the sentence left my lips, all knowledge of the past evaporated and I laughed quietly at my own words. What a silly thing to say, I thought. After forty-one years in this dear old body, the size of my breasts certainly shouldn't be news to me. I shook my head at my foolishness.

I was still laughing as I pulled on jeans and a sweatshirt. My mop of brown curls resisted the brush so I yanked it back and applied a scrunchie to hold it in place. A dab of lip gloss and I was ready to face the world of Saturday morning soccer.

Frankie's head popped back into the room. "Can we do McDonalds drive-through?" he asked.

"Sure," I answered, "but nothing too heavy. Don't want you throwing up Egg McMuffin all over the goalie."

"Oh, mom, that's gross!" He flashed me a look of twelve-year-old disgust. "Hurry up! I'll meet you at the car."

I took one more look in the mirror, tucked in a couple errant strands of hair and followed the sound of Frankie's footsteps.

The drive to McDonalds and on to his game was a preview of life with an adolescent. Somehow it seemed to be my fault that Frankie was too short, too slow, too clumsy and of course, fatherless. By the time we arrived at the field, I was delighted to relinquish him to the care and keeping of his coach. If I could have signed over custody, I would have done so on the spot.

I stopped the car briefly so that he would not have to walk with me, parked, and walked to the field. The trees on the east side offered shade and I found a spot to sit and a trunk to lean back upon. Two separate fields met at that point, and the rhythm of pre-game warm-ups lulled me into a state approaching sleep. Indeed, I might have dozed except for the frantic voice of a young girl from the field to the north. I looked up and watched as she clenched her hands and rocked from foot to foot.

"How could you forget to bring the orange slices, Daddy?" she fretted. "Everyone will hate me!"

Two strong arms reached out to steady her. "Oh, baby, I'm sorry," a gentle voice said. "I'll run over to the market right now and get some. Not to worry. I'll be there and back long before half time."

"Really, Daddy?"

"Absolutely, Kelly. Go back to your team. I'll take care of it."

He turned and looked down at me as soon as she left. "Well I'm in big trouble, aren't I?" he said.

I stood up and brushed the dirt off the seat my jeans. "I'd say you are. Sorry for listening in," I said.

"It would have been hard not to." He shook his head. "When Kelly gets upset the world knows."

"Well forgetting to bring oranges can be pretty upsetting to a kid. But like you said, you can get them here long before they are needed, so I would guess you'll be forgiven."

"Yeah. She is as quick to forgive, as she is to fall apart. Lucky for me. I haven't mastered this parent-in-charge thing yet. If I don't write it down, I don't get it done," he said. "I honestly don't know how my wife managed to do it all without a list."

"Is she traveling?" I asked, assuming the reason she was absent was divorce.

"No," he said softy. "She died last spring."

"I am so sorry," I replied, wishing I had not asked.

He nodded. "It is getting a little easier," he said. "I have a lot of help, my in-laws and a couple of my wife's good friends, but I'm trying to do as much of it myself as I can. And I guess I better get going before Kelly sees me here and falls apart again."

"Don't forget to buy a knife," I said.

"A knife?"

"The oranges have to be cut into pieces. In fact if you buy two knives, I'll help you cut the wedges."

"Thanks. It's a deal," he said and offered his hand. "Dick McBane. I teach history at Lord of Hosts High School."

"Ivy Smith," I said, "Ivy like the vine, Smith like, well I guess like all the other Smiths in the world."

He laughed. "You look familiar," he said.

"I teach at Early Start Nursery School, so if you have a toddler?"

"No. Kelly is the baby in the family." He looked toward the field where his daughter was attempting to move a soccer ball around several orange cones.

"Probably shouldn't tell her I called her that."

"No," I laughed, "probably not."

"So nursery school, huh? That has to require some pretty high energy, but I would guess it's enjoyable."

"Right on both counts. Tiring but fun. Could definitely pay better, but it gets me home before my son and I like that. Although after spending this morning listening to his royal grumpiness blame me for everything but the Peloponnesian War, I am not sure I will still think that is such a good idea when his hormones really start to flow."

We both laughed.

"What about Mr. Smith?"

"His hormones already flowed and he followed them." I turned away, embarrassed that I'd said that to a perfect stranger.

"He was a foolish man." The words were spoken gently.

I stole a quick look at his face. There was no mocking in his eyes. If anything there was a flash of sorrow or resolve. I could not tell for sure.

"Don't forget the knives," I answered.

"Not a chance," he replied.

He turned to leave and I watched as he walked across the field. An image flashed as I imagined his body lying beside me in bed, the arms that reached out to his child curled around me, holding me tight against him.

Holy crap, Ivy, I thought. I just met the man and I'm thinking about going to bed with him! The thought was terrifying and at the same time incredibly sensual. I breathed deeply and savored the sensations. A voice interrupted my fantasy.

"Hey, mom, my coach wants to talk to you."

There must be some kind of radar implanted in kids before birth, I thought. Sit down on a toilet or even think of sex, and they immediately materialize to demand your attention.

Frankie kicked a ball from foot to foot as he spoke. "I think coach is going to ask you to be a team mother. I think that would be pretty cool. Would it be cool with you, Mom?"

I groaned a silent groan. Just what I need, one more unpaid task to add to an already overly full day. Oh, well, I thought, perhaps this is divine intervention. Maybe someone up above figures I will be better off if I'm too busy to fantasize about sex with a total stranger.

"Yeah," I said smiling. "That would be cool."

I followed Frankie to a group of soccer players gathered on the opposite side of the field, where a man was showing them how to head the ball. "Keep your eyes on where you want the ball to land," he instructed in a patient voice, "not on the player who is running toward you."

"Hey coach," Frankie called out, "here's my mom."

His coach turned toward us and grinned. His body was tan and muscular and two grey eyes sparkled with pleasure. "Well, hello, Mrs. Smith. I'm Coach Larsen, Fred to you. And I think this just might be my lucky day. Usually people disappear when I send kids off to ask them to be a team parent. Might I assume that this is a yes?"

I rolled my eyes in mock resignation. "Yeah, you've got a victim this time. And please call me Ivy," I answered. "Mrs. Smith is my ex-husband's mother."

"Lucky me, Ivy," he said. He held out his right hand in thanks. The other hand held a soccer ball. When he tossed it to a player I noted with inappropriate satisfaction that there was no wedding ring and as his hand shook mine, I shivered with anticipation.

Oh great, I thought, blushing as he dropped my hand and turned to kick a ball back to one of the kids. It is not quite ten in the morning, and I have already lusted after two total strangers. Bet I'm not what the pollsters think of when they refer to the soccer mom vote.

"Anyway," I began, struggling for composure, "I'm glad to help. I mean after all, look at the work you do. Two practices a week and a game nearly every Saturday. You must love soccer. Did you play as a kid?"

"A little, well actually quite a lot all the way through college, but then work took over my life. For years I worked way too many hours to see the light of day, let alone a soccer field."

I laughed. "Been there, done that," I said. "So what changed?"

"I don't know exactly. Everything was going along pretty much as planned and then one day it hit me that I was no longer enjoying life. Best I can explain it is that one morning I woke up, took a good look at myself, and realized that I was always waiting for what might come next – the next day – the next year. It reminded me of something my dad used to say to my mom when we were shopping at K-Mart."

"What was that?"

"He said a person can waste a hell of a good life waiting for the blue light special. Seemed to me that was exactly what I was doing, so I changed."

I stood quietly as he turned away to yell to his team: "Go on over to the bench for some water. I'll be right there."

"And do you?" I asked. "Enjoy life more now that is?"

"Oh yes," he said with just the hint of a grin. "Life is definitely better."

"Makes sense to me," I said quietly.

He said, "See ya later, Ivy," and turned toward the group of children who waited for him.

I watched as he walked across the field with the sure gait of an athlete. An image flashed as I imagined his body lying beside me in bed, the arms that tossed soccer balls to his team curled around me, holding me tight against him. I breathed deeply and savored the sensations.

Who knew one small New Jersey town could be overflowing with such enticing men, I thought. What a delightful prospect.

"Fred," I called. He turned.

"I believe I am going to enjoy being a team parent," I said.

And I did.